Cycles of Destruction

Jason P. Crawford

FOREWORD

Mankind has always looked to the stars, seeking explanations for the burning lights in the sky. Some thought they were gods, or spirits watching over humanity from the great beyond. Eventually, mankind discovered that the stars were just like our own sun, but that did nothing to deter our fantasies. What might live amongst them? What ancient civilizations could be watching over us from afar?

At some point, we learned to differentiate the planets in our own system from those stars. This changed everything – no longer was Earth the only world in the universe. New imagination was sparked; what if there was life on other planets? What secrets could they hold? What if, someday, mankind could reach those planets, examine them, even set foot on them?

This novel is written in that spirit. Even now, as of this writing, people seek to colonize our neighbor planets, Venus and Mars, turning them into outposts of our civilization. Some see this development as the only defense our species has against a cataclysmic extinction event.

I want to thank all those who have ever looked to the sky, with their eyes, binoculars, telescopes, or other instruments, and wondered what might be there, wondered what it would be like if *we* were there.

ACKNOWLEDGMENTS

I want to recognize my wife, Cherrie, for her tireless work
in creating my covers and supporting my writing.

I also want to say thank you to my three sons: Ishmael,
Beowulf, and Odysseus. Daily they bring new perspectives
and new ideas into my life, and I am eternally grateful..

OCTOBER 17TH, 2015

"Dr. Riley!"

Jacob Riley looked up from the notes he was examining. His eyes squinted in the Antarctic sunlight; snow blindness was a real risk here, but his goggles made it hard for him to read. He slipped them back over his eyes as the young woman, a graduate student on-station with an academic program, trundled through the thin layer of snow covering the ice.

The older man scowled at the student. "What is it? I have more of these analyses to deal with." He rolled his shoulders and neck, trying to work out the stiffness. "As if any of this crap matters anyway."

Her breath pumped in and out as she spoke. "Dr. Riley, we found…something. We need you to come take a look at it."

Jacob's eyebrow crooked. "What? Did you find a baby seal or something? We're in a Godforsaken climatology station in the goddamn Antarctic. What could possibly be so important that you had to…"

"Just come with me." Behind her goggles, Jacob saw that her eyes were wide, almost panicked. "We need you to come see this *now*."

The urgency in her voice startled him. "…All right." He went into the nearby tent, drew on his heavier coat, snow goggles, boots. "What is it?"

Several other team members were now watching the pair, pausing in their work.

"This way, Doctor." The grad student turned away, heading toward one of the excavation sites the team used to dig for and analyze ice samples. Once they were away from the main group, Jacob reached for her shoulder.

"Okay, Genesis, what's going on?"

Genesis did not turn nor stop walking. "Everything was normal, and we were taking another ice core sample, when we hit something."

"What? A gas pocket? A buried meteorite?" Jacob shook his head. "You know we don't have time for nonsense around here. Just tell me what happened."

"I'd really rather not say, Dr. Riley. We…we aren't sure what it is and I don't want to…" She paused for a minute. "…I don't want to sound crazy."

"Look, I really don't like surprises." Jacob sped up so he was walking next to Genesis, his feet making crunching sounds in the snow as he overtook her. "What do you think it is?"

"Well…" she licked her lips, which were covered in balm to protect them from the cold. "It…it seems like some sort of …artificial object." She paused. "And we have no idea where it came from."

Jacob stopped, mid-stride. "Is this some kind of joke, Genesis? Because if it is…"

The young woman turned and grabbed hold of one of Jacob's hands, tugging it with her. "It's just over here. Come on!"

Jacob found himself getting excited as he continued to follow the student. *What if she's right? What if there really is some sort of …no, it couldn't be. But what if it is? Imagine! Imagine what that would mean! I could finally -*

"It's right here." Genesis led the chief climatologist over a small rise. "We covered it up so that no one else would see it." She laughed, but there was a nervous energy behind the sound. "I guess it wouldn't get damaged if we left it out in the cold, though, huh?'

"I suppose not, if it's been here for a while already. I guess we'll see." They crested the rise. For a moment, the glare blinded Jacob, and he shaded his eyes once more to allow them to adjust. Below, about a hundred yards from their position, was a small group, four members strong. They had scientific and excavation equipment: thermometers, borers, and ice core extractors, and they were surrounding a tarp stretched tight over something on the ground, with stakes holding down the corners. The researchers were huddled together, murmuring and whispering, but they snapped back to attention as Jacob arrived.

"All right, take it off." Jacob motioned with his hands. "I want to see it."

Without a word, the assembled students and technicians each pulled up a stake and took a corner of the tarp into their hands. They walked backward, revealing the secret hidden beneath.

The artifact was a cylinder, about a foot long and three inches in diameter. It was clearly metal, silver in color with script carved into its surface; the carvings were neat and clean, laser-cut rather than hand-made. There was some sort of strange transparent material, pitted in places and burned off in others, that sheathed the metal. Jacob walked toward it and knelt down beside it.

"Dr. Riley! Shouldn't you…"

Jacob shook his head, and the other man fell silent. With slow-moving, careful hands, he brushed ice and snow off the surface of the cylinder and leaned in closer.

"Oh my God." Then, louder, "This thing is…could be a housing of some kind." He traced the seam in the metal with his finger. "There might be something inside it." He panned his gaze across the small crowd, trying to conceal the excitement he felt straining in his voice. "We need to get this out of here and back to the States for examination."

"Yes, Doctor. I'll get on the radio to our people." Genesis started running back toward the camp as Jacob turned to the others.

"The rest of you, I need shipping materials and a manifest written up for this immediately. I'll be taking the…the object back myself."

"Wait a minute!" One of the researchers, a middle-aged man named Rick, stepped forward. "We found this. We should get credit for finding it." He crossed his arms. "This could be the biggest scientific discovery in history that we've got here, and –"

Murmurs of assent rose from the other three until Jacob silenced them with his glare. "We don't *have* anything yet, Mr. Cruz." He raised his voice. "This goes for all of you. If you run around telling everyone that you 'found an alien artifact' and you turn out to be wrong, then we lose credibility and you risk starting a panic. That's why I'm going with it and you're staying here." Then he chuckled. "Well, that and I'm the one with the PhD. When you finish with your thesis, Mr. Cruz, *you* can write the journal articles and get them published."

Half-hearted laughter from the workers.

Riley turned back to the cylinder, caressing it once more with his gloved fingers. "Did we get samples of the ice that was surrounding the object?"

"…Yes, sir." Rick brought up the container which housed the sample. "It was properly prepared before we went back in after the artifact. Cataloged, tagged. We should be able to tell how long it's been buried in there."

Jacob nodded. "Well done. All right, not a word about this to any of the others, no matter how well you think they might keep a secret. For those of you looking for credit for the discovery, the worst thing that could happen is the government swooping in here and seizing control of the entire site." He looked at Rick as he spoke.

After a few seconds, Rick nodded, followed by the others. "Not a word."

Jesse, another graduate student with thinning black hair peeking out from under his parka, nudged Rick in the ribs. "As if anyone would believe us anyway!"

"After all, it's probably nothing. Probably just some science experiment some kid launched off that ended up in the Antarctic. On a weather balloon or something. Right?"

Nods and assent all around.

"Okay, then. I'll wait here while you all get the packaging materials. Genesis should have already gotten in contact with McMurdo and I'll be on the next flight back to Christchurch. Any questions?"

Headshakes.

"Get to it, then."

The group dispersed, heading back through the Antarctic wastes to the Amudsen-Scott station. Jacob watched them leave, then his face relaxed, allowing the excitement to show through.

"My God." He resumed his kneeling position, bringing his face closer to the cylinder. "What if they're right? What if …?" He brushed his gloved hand over the burnt shielding. "Looks like it's some sort of …I don't know...hydrocarbon based polymer, maybe. Almost like a riot shield." He poked the jagged edges where the coating had been burned. "This metal…it looks like steel. Or titanium, maybe, or an alloy. No telling until we get it to a lab, I guess." He traced his fingers over the markings. "These…these look almost like letters. And words. Yes! They have spaces and what seems like…"

"Dr. Riley?"

Jacob straightened up, his face suddenly warm underneath the thick clothes he wore. His fellow researchers had returned with packing materials and were looking at him, expressions difficult to see under their hoods and goggles.

"All right." Jacob knelt down again and picked up the cylinder in both hands. It was heavy for its size, at least ten pounds, and lifting it elicited a grunt of effort from the scientist as he extracted it from the snow and walked it over to the shipping container. It thudded amongst the foam before he packed it tight and locked it in. Standing, he nodded and looked at his colleagues.

"Okay, then. Let's get this going. The plane should be here soon, I hope." The group walked back to the station, most of them heading inside to warm themselves up after their extended expedition in the Antarctic cold; even during summer, one had to be careful.

Jacob, however, went to gather up his equipment and gear for the ride back to civilization. He laughed to himself. *At least I don't have to serve out my full sentence. Much rather be back in the States than here at the bottom of the world.* His eyes strayed several times to the case, part of him wanting to take it out, examine it, but he resisted the temptation. *Wouldn't make a difference anyway – need good gear to check something like this out and we just don't have that here.*

A few minutes of getting his notes ready for the climatologist who would replace Riley as project lead led up to the arrival of the transport aircraft. Jacob shoved the last of his equipment and clothing into his bag and headed out to the airstrip.

"What's going on?" called one of the analysts. "Where are you going, Dr. Riley?"

"Nothing to worry about, just a personal emergency. Dr. Taliesin is going to take over the remainder of the summer projects. He'll be here tomorrow or the day after. Good luck!"

The analyst seemed flabbergasted as Jacob hopped on board the plane. The climatologist passed by several workers offloading supplies and returning with research materials to be cataloged. One of them passed by his seat.

"Good morning, Doctor. Excited to be heading home?"

Jacob Riley smiled, his hand touching the container beside his seat. He nodded.
"Yes. Very excited."

OCTOBER 31, 2015

A young boy came running around the corner, brandishing a plastic sword and adjusting his armor. "Dad! Come on! You're supposed to be getting your Halloween costume on!"

"In a minute, in a minute. I need to finish these lesson plans." Cameron Mitchell stood up from his laptop and office desk. He stretched, making a yawn that seemed as if he had not slept in weeks, and looked down at his six year old boy.

"What's the rush anyway, M&M?" He leaned to the side, tousling his son's hair. "It's not even dark yet."

"I *know*." Mike Mitchell paced around the small office dressed in a medieval knight costume. "But I love seeing you in your Halloween costume. It's *awesome*. Please? Pretty please?" Mike clasped his hands together and did his best to give his father goo-goo, Puss-in-Boots eyes. Mike just laughed; the contrast between the eyes and the armored helmet was too much for him to take.

Mike deflated a bit. "Why are you laughing at me? I just want to go trick-or-treating with you."

Cameron knelt down and hugged his son. "Hey, I'm not laughing *at* you, Mike. I'm laughing because you're cute, because I love you. You want to go trick-or-treating?"

Mike's eyes shone. "Yeah! All right!"

"Have you taken your medication?"

Mike rolled his eyes. "Yes, Dad. I don't forget that, you know! Mom made sure I wouldn't."

At the mention of Cameron's wife, both went silent for a few seconds. Cameron cleared his throat. "And you remember why it's so important that you don't forget?"

Mike scrunched up his face as he thought. "Because…because you don't want me slamming my head against the floor?" He leveled serious eyes on his father. "Don't worry, Dad. I don't want to do that either."

Cameron nodded, wiping away embryonic tears with the heel of his hand. "Okay then, I'll just put on my suit and we can get going."

"Yaaaay!" Mike danced around the room, pumping his arms up and down as Cameron exited. *Kids. I remember when I got that excited about Halloween.* He opened his closet, eyes lingering on the Army dress uniform, festooned with ribbons and medals, that still hung there even though his discharge had been over a year ago, then pulled down his costume. He smiled again, remembering the day they had gone shopping for these.

Cameron had been tired; it had been a long day at work and his son had been playing in an impromptu kiddie football game that ran late into the evening. When it was over (Mike's team had won in a close match), Mike asked if they were going to celebrate like they sometimes did.

Cameron had forced a smile. "Sure, M&M. What did you want to go do?"

His son had thought for a few seconds, then threw his arms up in his booster seat and shouted, "Let's go get Halloween costumes!"

So they had gone to the big Halloween stores, looking through the costume sets, and Mike had picked out a very well-done medieval knight costume, complete with helmet, shield, and sword. After two hours of searching, though, they hadn't found anything for Cameron. To be fair, Cameron had found several things – a pirate, a samurai, even a nice forest-god costume—but Mike had vetoed each one, saying they weren't "right."

"Hey, Mike," he had said, rubbing his face and suppressing a yawn. "I'm really tired; maybe we can find mine later?" He had glanced into the mirror as he spoke.

Mike's face had fallen. "Dad…" Tears had welled up in his eyes, overshadowing the joy which had shone there moments ago. "You need to have a Halloween costume."

"Why, big man?"

"Because Halloween was Momma's favorite."

There it was. Cameron's wife, Suzanne, had been a huge fan of Halloween, and had always turned it into a big production. No one was able to escape her makeup brush come October 31st; she would spend months planning each costume, and a significant portion of their budget would be spent on prosthetics, fabrics, and paints.

"All right, buddy." Cameron had nodded. "We'll keep looking." At this point, he was willing to pick up the next thing that fit, no matter what Mike said, when…

"Right there, Dad! Right there!"

Cameron had whipped his head to the left; there was a thrift store, locally owned, with a big sign reading *Halloween Specials! 50% off!*

And in the window…was Godzilla, looming over a miniature cityscape with Lego figures running in terror. The same Godzilla costume that Cameron was now forcing himself into, complete with giant head, eyeholes in the neck, and detachable, button-on tail. It was big, it was heavy…and his son had adored it, so they had bought it.

Costuming complete, Cameron stomped his way out of the bedroom, making big growly sounds and raising his arms at his son. Mike squealed, pulling out his costume sword as if to fight the giant reptilian monster. With a lunge, Godzilla surged forward and swooped up the miniscule knight in his arms.

"Dad!" Mike squirmed in his father's arms. "Lemme go!"

"Dad? There is no 'Dad' here! There is only…Godzilla!" Cameron started tickling his son under his armpits, leading to increased squeals and squirms.

"No! No!"

"Godzilla not eat little boy?" Cameron held his son for another moment before lowering him to the ground. "Well…all right." Cameron let Mike go; the boy was still giggling. "Are you ready to head out?"

"You bet!" Mike ran into the living room and grabbed his pumpkin-shaped Halloween basket. "We're gonna get *tons* of candy this year, huh, Dad?"

"Tons and tons, kiddo. Go buckle in; I'll be right there."

Mike sprinted out of the front door and towards the car. Cameron watched him go, smiling even as his eyes misted up. He turned toward the family portrait on the wall and reached out one hand, grazing the image of his wife. Her beautiful face and dark hair were frozen in printer ink, but he couldn't help but return the soft smile.

"As long as I have him, you're never really gone." He kissed his fingertips and touched them to her mouth, then headed to the car to join his son. Mike was already buckled in, his sword in the seat next to him, smiling his gap-toothed grin and watching his father.

"Okay, M&M, what do you think?" Cameron took off his costume head and tail, stowing them in the passenger seat. "Should we hit that neighborhood we went to last year, or should we try somewhere new first?"

Mike's eyes went wide, like an owl's reflecting the moonlight. "Is that the neighborhood that had the house with the really spooky zombies in the front yard and the ghosts in the trees?"

Cameron laughed as he turned the key in the ignition. "You mean the one that had the guy hiding in the zombie costume on the bench that jumped out and scared us half to death?"

"Yeah!" Mike's head was nodding up and down so much that it made his seat shake.

"That's the one."

Mike clapped his hands. "Can we go there, Dad? Please please please?"

"Okay then." Cameron turned on the satellite radio as he backed the car out of his driveway. "Now, what're the rules?"

Mike took a deep breath, like a performer before his solo. He extended one finger at a time, ticking off the points. "No eating candy until you've had the chance to check it out. Say 'thank you,' no matter how much or how little candy I get. Don't ask for more." He beamed a smile at his father.

Cameron frowned. "There's one more rule, you know."

Mike's smile faltered. "…What?"

"Have fun!" Cameron's grin burst forth, and Mike laughed.

"You scared me for a second, there, Dad! I thought you were mad at me!"

"Nah. Not today, M&M. Now, let's go get some candy!"

"Yeah!"

~~~

Halloween night had been a rousing success. Mike's favorite house had outdone itself; in addition to the creepy zombies and flying ghosts, the owner had hidden inside of a fake grave setup under the ground and shrouded by a fog machine. Mike had tiptoed up the walkway, expecting to be scared at any moment, but the man had waited until the boy was on his way back with his candy to lunge out of the ground and grab Mike's ankle. The child had screamed loud enough to shatter glass, and Snickers and Kit-Kats had scattered everywhere, but when the man had climbed out of the grave and taken off his mask all the fear gave way to laughter and joy.

Now, Mike was asleep in his chair, his mouth slack, cheeks smooth, and his pumpkin of goodies was propped at his side with his sword and shield resting atop it. Cameron kept glancing in the rear view mirror, marveling at the blessing that was his.

I wish you were here to see him right now, Suze. You'd be proud of our little guy.
~~~

His favorite radio station changed over from music to news. Cameron rolled his eyes and moved to turn on his CD player.

"…the entire staff of the Antarctic research facility were found dead this morning."

Cameron paused. *What the hell?*

The talk host continued. "According to my sources, the pilot of the supply plane that found them was taken into custody for questioning, but the FBI has no other leads at this time." The voice on the radio gave a mirthless chuckle. "See, what I don't understand is *why?* I mean, what do they do down there? Melt ice, see how fast ice is melting? Hey, guys, how's that ice doing? You know? Easy to make fun of, but then, you find out that the scientists and staff were found all over the complex, having just fallen over and died in the middle of their work." Another sad laugh. "It's like God just said, 'Hey, you're right, they *are* pointless,' and just wiped them out." A pause. "So far, there has been no statement about the incident, but I'm sure that they're just pissing in their pants trying to figure this shit out up at the White House."

"Holy hell." Cameron continued listening, but the host turned to mocking reports of the Mars Omega operation and its selection of the first teams of potential Mars colonists, so he turned it off, shaking his head. "Crazy damn world. Whole station just gets killed like that? Who does something like that?" He shook his head, sighing.

The headlights of his Toyota lit up the bumpy road to his house, and he turned in. He coasted down the path, avoiding the potholes and dips that come with unpaved roads, and guided the vehicle into his driveway. Parking the car, he turned off the ignition, opened the rear passenger door, and extracted his son from the back seat. Mike murmured and turned his face into his father's chest, a sight that caused Cameron's heart to melt once again.

"It's all right, little man." Cameron kissed his son on the forehead as he laid Mike in his bed and tucked him in. "Daddy's here. Everything's going to be all right."

Mike stirred, shifted, settled. A sleepy mumble escaped his lips. "Love you, Momma."

A pang tore at Cameron's heart; he switched on his son's Mickey Mouse nightlight, casting a soft orange glow across the room. "Goodnight, Mike. Momma loves you too."

JOURNAL OF JACOB RILEY
OCTOBER 31ST

The dreams are getting worse. I haven't been sleeping, and I...I've been having them when I'm awake now. I'll just lose an hour and there she'll be, staring at me.

I'm still not sure what it all means, but it's bad. God, is it bad. I can't write it here in case this gets lost; if the wrong people find out...but what is it? I'm not even sure.

Heard it on the radio today, but I'm not really surprised. Everyone else is dead. All of them, without an explanation. Not that simple. Coincidence doesn't stretch that far. Never has.

God, I need sleep. Never thought I'd be running like this. Guess it could be worse. Could be dead. Could have had my head taken off. No. Can't think like that. Have to move.

I need to find out who's behind this. Or what. Need to find a way to get this out in the open. But...what if I'm wrong? What if I tell the wrong person? God. Need to get out of town. Hope all those crazy TV shows I used to watch with those criminals off the grid weren't entirely bullshit.

Shit. This still doesn't seem real. Haven't had a chance to shave in days. Keep seeing guns everywhere. People staring at me. Even the kids seem like they're watching me. Can't sleep. Keep dreaming of Genesis, Rick, everyone, all dead. Must've been the same people.

I'm rambling again. Need coffee. Gonna get on the bus, head north. Get away from here. Hope that the dreams don't happen again. Sometimes it feels like I'm losing track of what I'm doing; I keep waking up in places that I don't remember going to, places I don't know why I'm there.

And Genesis. Genesis in the red dirt. She keeps trying to tell me something, but I'm not understanding. Every day, it's a little clearer, like she's relearning the language...but it's just a dream, right?

God help me.

NOVEMBER 1ST, 8:26 A.M.

"Get up, Dad! It's time to get up!"

Cameron cracked his eyes open; sunlight was streaming in through his bedroom windows, and his son was straddling him, with his hands on his father's cheeks, staring into his eyes and waiting for him to wake up. When he saw Cameron's eyelids retract, Mike grinned and bounced up and down.

"Good morning, Dad! Can I have my Halloween candy now?"

"First…you…need…to...stop…bouncing…on …me!"

"Oh." Mike stopped and rolled to the side; he was wearing pajamas with rocket ships on them, buttoned up to the very top. "So? Can I?"

Cameron rubbed his face. "What time is it?"

"I don't know."

"Have you eaten anything yet?"

Mike's smile widened. "Nope! I didn't touch the candy, just like I promised." He nodded for emphasis.

Cameron laughed. "I meant, have you eaten any real food? Like, I don't know, a sandwich? Cereal? Something?"

Mike shook his head.

"All right." Cameron rolled over and out of bed, slipping on his housecoat and sliding into his slippers. "Your mom would kill me if I let you have your candy before you at least ate some breakfast, so how about I fix us both an omelet?"

Mike grimaced. "Only if mine doesn't have any vegetables."

Cameron rolled his eyes. "All right, crazy man. No vegetables. Except tomatoes."

Mike considered, then nodded. "Deal."

"All right. Let me brush my teeth and use the bathroom, then we're set."

Mike shifted his weight from one foot to the other, impatient for his father to finish his morning routine. Cameron noticed, and took great pains to brush his teeth slowly, exaggerating his efforts to rinse his mouth out by holding the water in one cheek for several seconds, then the other, then gargling, then...

"Dad! Come *on!*"

Cameron spat the water into the sink and dabbed at his face with the washcloth. "All right, all right. Let's go have breakfast."

~~~

"What're we gonna do today, Dad?"

Cameron stood behind the sink, scrubbing the remains of their breakfast dishes. Mike had already dug into his Halloween prizes, and wrappers of Hershey's Kisses and packets of Reese's Pieces lay in a small pile at the table beside him.

"I was thinking that we might head down to L.A. today, maybe hit the zoo or the science center." He looked over at his son. "Whaddaya think?"

Mike considered. "It's been a while since we were at the zoo. I'd really like to get to see the elephants this time! Last time they were hiding and I didn't get to see any." He smiled. "Elephants are my favorite animals, you know."

Cameron finished washing the dishes and began to dry them. "Really? What happened to octopuses and squid?"

Mike waved off his father's question. "I still like them. But! Can I tell you something?"

"Shoot."

"Elephants actually hold funerals for their family members. They're sad when someone they know dies, just like people.." A somber moment of silence, then: "Isn't that awesome!" Mike's voice took on the character of a professor giving a lesson. "There aren't any elephant graveyards or anything like that, but elephants are the only species other than humans that care about their dead."
~~~

Cameron blinked. "Wow. That is pretty cool, actually. Where did you learn that?."

Mike shrugged. "I watched a video about elephants at school on my tablet."

Cameron patted Mike on the head and his son beamed. "The zoo it is then." He glanced at the clock on the stove. "If we leave now, we should be able to get plenty of time to see the elephants and everything else that's there."

"Yaaay!" Mike ran toward his room, bumping into the corner and continuing on his way. "I'll get my Explorer's bag!"

"You do that, M&M. I'll get our food and stuff ready." Cameron smiled at his son's exuberance. Ever since his wife had died, little things like a trip to the zoo with his son had been what had kept him going until the wound scabbed over. "Remember to bring one friend with you in the car for the trip."

"Okay, Dad!" Cameron set to work making peanut butter and honey sandwiches for the two of them, adding bananas for extra flavor. Two juice boxes apiece, apple for him and fruit punch for his son, and a container of fresh grapes and carrot sticks finished the ensemble. By the time he was done, Mike was standing at the door, his Thundercats backpack filled with his computer tablet, his favorite homemade robot figurine, and a stuffed penguin that was peeking its head out the top. The two nodded to each other and exited to the car.

"All right." Cameron pulled out the case of DVDs that he kept in the vehicle for long trips. "What is your viewing pleasure today, monsieur?"

"I'm not 'ma-sur'." Mike thumped his chest. "I'm Michael Montgomery Mitchell!"

Cameron laughed. "I just meant, what movie do you want?"

"Oh." Mike considered, looking up at the ceiling and rubbing his chin with his thumb and forefinger. "How about…Land Before Time? The one with Chomper and the island?"

"Ah, a classic choice. Very well, sir." Cameron slid the disk into the car's DVD player and started it up, checking his mirrors and switching on the sound for the movie. "It'll take us about an hour and a half to get there, if traffic is all right."

"Okay, Dad. Can we get a hamburger on the way?"

"We'll see, kiddo. Hamburgers cost money, you know, and we can't just get one every time we go out." He shook his head. "It adds up. Plus they're not all that good for you to eat *all* the time."

"*Please*?" Mike held his hands in classic prayer position. "Hamburgers are my *favorite*. I like them with…"

"With just meat and cheese, I know." Cameron shook his head, then turned to face the rear of the Toyota and started backing up. "If you want a burger, M&M, you'll have to have it with lettuce and pickles. I know you can handle that."

Mike clapped his hands in glee. "Okay! Sounds great! Let's go!"

~~~

Jacob Riley, formerly one of the chief climatologists at the United States' Antarctic Research Station, was on a Greyhound bus heading north. He was bundled in a large Army-surplus coat, and with his very heavy stubble, weary eyes, and drawn face, he more resembled a career vagrant than a highly educated man of science. In his lap was a lunch container, brown and about two feet long, zipped up and attached to his hand by a thin length of chain. The bus was nearly empty, and that was the only reason he had allowed himself to drift off to sleep; his eyes were closed, and he snored, his cheek pressed against the window with a thin trail of drool. Even in his sleep, his brows were knitted, and he tossed, murmured. On her way back from the restroom, a young lady with red hair and green eyes shook her head and stepped as far to the side of the aisle as possible when she passed him.

In the front of the bus, an older woman nodded in response to something on the other end of her phone conversation, her eyes hidden by sunglasses and a large hat. She put her phone away and looked toward the sleeping scientist.
~~~

~~~

Mike tossed his wrapper into the trash can between the front and back seats. "Dad, can we have another hamburger on our way back?"

Cameron glanced in the rear-view mirror at his son, rolling his eyes. "Another hamburger? Have you turned into the Hamburgler or something?"

Mike crinkled his nose. "The Hamburgler? Who is that?"

Cameron sighed. "Great. You're making your old man feel…well…old, son. Thanks."

Mike giggled. "You're not old, Dad. I know people who are *way* older than you. Like Mr. McCowsky."

Cameron returned the laugh. "Yeah, Mr. McCowsky does seem like he's seen a few years, doesn't he?"

Mike nodded. "He says that he's been around since Noah's Ark and stuff."

"Do you believe him?"

"Nah." Mike took another drink of his chocolate shake. "There's no way that…oops!" The shake slipped out of Mike's hands, sending chocolaty milk-stuff cascading over the boy's lap, down the seat, and onto the floor of the Toyota.

"Dammit!" Cameron bit back a lecture, searching around for napkins or a towel, eyes darting between the road and the surrounding seating areas until he found them. "Here, Mike." He extended a handful back toward his son until he felt
~~~

them taken. "Clean yourself up. You okay?" Cameron glanced toward the back seat.

"I'm fine...DAD LOOKOUT!!" Mike's eyes went wide with terror, and Cameron snapped his attention back to the front. A Greyhound bus in their lane spun out of control, colliding with two other vehicles ahead of them and sending up a plume of flame as it flipped onto one side and skidded to a stop in the middle of the road. Cameron slammed on his brakes and brought his car to a rough stop on the shoulder. He took a few deep breaths to settle his pounding heart. A quick glance at the scene revealed that no one was crawling away from the wreckage.

"You stay here, Mike. Don't unlock the door for anyone, do you understand?"

Mike's face was frightened, his eyes teary. "Where are you going, Dad? Don't leave me!"

Cameron unbuckled his seatbelt and turned around. "Hey. M&M. Look at me." He waited until his son held his gaze. "There are people in that bus, and some of them might still be alive. They could be hurt and not be able to get out, but if someone doesn't save them, they could die. I need to see if I can help them. Okay?"

Mike took a shuddering breath, then nodded, but the fear did not leave his voice. "O...okay, Dad."

Tousling his son's hair one more time, Cameron got out of the car, locked the door, and ran to the crash site. The smell of gasoline fumes and burnt steel and rubber filled the air, driving some gawkers back into the relative safety of their vehicles. Several bystanders were on their cellphones, reporting the accident to the authorities, and others hovered over the scene like vultures, taking photos to upload to YouTube or Facebook. Cameron circled around the fallen bus, trying to get a look at the damage, see if there were any survivors.

His heart sank and his gorge rose.

The driver was dead; there was a huge crack in the windshield where his head had slammed into it and red and pink fluid was oozing over the glass. A woman was near him, sprawled over the guard railing, with her sunglasses broken and her neck crooked at an impossible angle that made her look like some sort of marionette. A pair of young girls, maybe Mike's age or a little older, were holding each other, and were impaled together on a broken guardrail—one through the heart, the other through the head. Cameron closed his eyes a moment to shut out the horror.

Then he heard a ragged breath and a cough from inside.

"Hey! Get me some help over here!" Cameron sprinted to the bus, wrenching open the hatch on the roof and ducking inside. Acrid smoke now filled the interior of the bus, and Cameron covered his face with his shirt to try to filter some of it out.

"Hello?! Is someone in here?" His eyes were watering, but he resisted the urge to wipe for fear of shoving ash and smoke into them. He squinted and blinked, trying to clear the surreal, watery quality from the world.

"Help…" The voice was a wheeze, almost indistinguishable from the crackle of the fire and the sparks of electricity.

Moving to where he had heard the voice, Cameron saw a young woman, red-haired, cut up and bloody, but alive and looking around, holding one arm to her face to keep the smoke out. It seemed she had been shielded from the worst by the person who had been thrown on top of her—a middle-aged man, wearing a broken length of chain on his wrist and a very thick hand-me-down Army coat.

"Hold on!" Cameron rolled the dead man off of her, then grabbed hold of the woman; she groaned but wrapped her arms around him as he boosted her out of the aisle. "We have to get you out of here. The bus is on fire." Step by step he eased her through the skewed landscape of the toppled vehicle, reminding himself each step that he needed to move carefully. *If she has internal injuries, I could kill her, but if the bus explodes…*

He stepped on a piece of metal; it slipped out from under his foot and he stumbled. The woman he was carrying screamed as he tightened his grip to keep her from falling.

"Hey, hey, it's all right." He tried to keep his voice soothing, but it was difficult; the smoke was impeding his breathing…and she felt *heavy*. "Hey,

I'm Cameron, Cameron Mitchell. I'm going to get you out of here, okay? What's your name?"

"Stephanie Rhodes."

"Okay, Stephanie. Just hold on and we'll…"

"Look, can we hurry this up?" The woman coughed up bloody phlegm and tightened her grip on Cameron's shoulders. "I'd really like to *not* die on this damn bus, if that's okay with you."

Cameron laughed, then coughed, then laughed again. "Don't worry, we're almost there." And they were; within moments, Cameron had returned to the open hatch he had slipped in through. A crowd of other Samaritans had surrounded the hatch, and they reached in to help the young woman out of the bus and to safety. As they lifted her free, Cameron stepped over the edge and planted his feet on solid ground again.

He heard another car door slam as he bent over, coughing smoke fumes from his lungs and crawling away from the wreckage. Police and ambulance sirens were sounding in the distance, getting louder and louder by the moment. When he was able, he looked around at the gathered civilians and nodded. *We should be okay now.*

Cameron stumbled back toward his car; his son was sitting in the back, strapped in, and Mike waved at his father through the window when he saw him. The boy's face lost its smile when he saw the soot stains and bloodshot eyes before him, and he rolled his window down a crack.

"Are you okay, Dad?"

Cameron nodded and leaned against the side of the car. "I'll be…*cough*…I'll be fine, M&M. Don't worry."

Mike nodded and zipped up his Thundercat bag, grunting as he lowered it to the car floor. "What happened?"

"I don't know, big man." Cameron looked back toward the wreckage. "Someone got into a hell of an accident, though. Bus went over. Lots of people are…"

Mike's eyes were wide. "Are they dead, Dad?"

Cameron closed his eyes. "Yeah. Yeah, some of them."

"Whoa." Mike looked forward, through the windshield, then back at his father. "How did you get all dirty and stuff?"

"In a minute, Mike." Cameron watched as the police cruisers and emergency vehicles began pulling up. Several paramedics lifted Stephanie into the back of an ambulance; she looked at him over the oxygen mask on her face and waved in his direction before she disappeared. "I need to go talk to these guys and help them out a little bit, tell them what I saw. I'll tell you everything once we get out of here, okay?"

"Okay. Dad?"

"Yeah?"

"Can you turn the movie back on?"

Cameron smiled. "Sure. No problem."

"Thanks!"

In moments, the video was restored. The paramedics insisted on checking Cameron out, and, after a few moments, cleared him to speak to a uniformed, aging police officer. His much younger partner took notes, glancing from one to the other and clicking his pen.

"So, what did you see happen?"

Cameron rubbed his face. "The bus turned on its side, like someone had tried to make a really sharp turn with it and sent it skidding. Something caught on fire as it slid down the road."

The officer nodded. "You went in?"

"Yes. I had to see if there were any survivors. There was a fire, but the bus seemed mostly intact, so…"

"Were you certain that anyone had survived?"

Cameron's brows knitted together. "Umm…no. How could I be?"

"Sir, I respect your bravery, but that was a damn fool thing to do." The officer's face was stolid, immobile, but his words stung.

"Excuse me?"

The cop pointed back to the Toyota, where Mike sat watching his film. "What would've happened to him if you'd gotten yourself killed in there? If the whole thing went up and he had to watch his own father get charbroiled because he went in to save someone who might not have even needed saving?" Color flushed the older man's face as his voice rose, and Cameron took a step back.

"Do you have any idea what something like that can do to a kid? Because I do."

The officer's partner tapped him on the shoulder. "Jensen, maybe we'd better not…"

A moment of tense silence, then Jensen nodded. "All right. We have your contact information and your statement. If we need anything else, we'll let you know. Have a nice day, Mr. Mitchell." With that, he walked back to his patrol car. Jensen's partner shrugged.

"Sorry about that, sir."

Cameron shook his head. "No, it's not your fault. He's right, I guess, isn't he? I guess I didn't think about what might have happened to my son if something horrible had gone wrong."

The officer nodded and put a hand on Cameron's shoulder for a moment. "Drive safe, and take care. We'll be in touch if we need anything."

Cameron trudged back toward his car; as he approached, he could see Mike's face first, looking down into the seat, maybe, or his lap. His eyes flicked upward, met his father's, and then frenzied activity as his arms and hands moved. Cameron's brow wrinkled, and he walked up to his son's window.

"Whatcha doing, M&M?"

Mike's backpack lay beneath the boy's feet, with the zip half undone. "I was just trying to get Peeky!" He hugged his penguin to his chest. "I was feeling a little worried, so I needed a penguin-snuggle."

Cameron's suspicious look melted. "All right. I don't think that we can make it to the zoo today. Would it be okay if we headed back home, maybe had a movie night with popcorn, pick up some take-out food...?" Seeing his son's eyebrows rise, Cameron hurried on. "It's just that I'm really beat, now, big man. Not sure how much fun I'd be at the zoo, you know?" He leaned closer. "We could get ice cream..."

Mike looked his father over, then nodded. "Well...okay, Dad. But can we go tomorrow?"

Cameron snorted a laugh. "Working tomorrow, kiddo. But we'll go next weekend. Promise. Fair deal?"

"Fair deal."

INTERLUDE

Identity verified. Please give mission status report.

"We didn't find it."

Clarify. The agent said he was on the bus.

"He was. The cylinder is missing."

Explain. What are the most probable scenarios?

"Several civilian personnel arrived before the emergency crews. It is possible that one of them found the object before we were able to get on-site. The agent did not survive the crash, so she could not take possession of it."

Unfortunate. We must locate the cylinder. Present suggestions.

"We have records of all the civilians and emergency personnel who were present. It is a simple matter to obtain their addresses and other information. Determining which, if any, has the object…"

What about the one who entered the bus?

"Possible but unlikely. Our information shows that Cameron Mitchell is ex-Special Forces, enlisted at 18 and retired after 20 years. He was not observed carrying the cylinder as he carried out Ms. Rhodes."

Focus on the others first, then.

"I shall. What resources are being allocated to make sure that we accomplish our task?"

Emergency authorizations are engaged. The contents of the cylinder cannot be made public. If it has been accessed, then time is precious.

"I know."

Several seconds pass.

"Do we have any word yet on how it got here?"

Not your concern. Make sure the cylinder is reacquired, or the consequences could be disastrous.

"I understand."

NOVEMBER 2ND, 10:57 A.M.

3rd period ended, and Cameron Mitchell slumped into his seat. He rubbed his sore neck and took a long drink of water with two Extra-Strength Tylenol gelcaps. He laughed at himself.

"Must be getting old there, Mitchell. Back in the Army, carrying someone out of a burning bus would have been par for the course, no problem." He looked down at his body, filled with aches and bruises from the brief but harrowing ordeal of yesterday. "Guess not anymore."

After a second or two, he stirred, reached under his desk, and dug into his lunchbox for his sandwich, juice, and orange. A sad smile passed over his face.

I miss my salads. His eyes glimmered with tears, before he laughed at himself and wiped them away. "Stupid little things like that. Stupid little things like salads and tea and notes on the fridge."

His eyes moved up, looking past the ceiling. "God, I miss you so much."

As he ate, Cameron scanned through news articles on the Internet. Flipping to local news, he searched for anything about the accident of the previous day.

"There you are…" He blinked, rubbed his eyes, looked more closely. "What the hell?"

His eyes dug through the text in front of him, unbelieving. According to the article, the accident had occurred as the result of a blown tire…and there were no survivors.

Cameron pinched himself. It hurt.

"No…there should be something about Stephanie. She was fine. Did they miss her?" His fingers tapped at the keyboard. "Maybe it was a bad reporting job." A few more minutes of searching got him the names of the closest hospitals to the accident site, including phone numbers. He was about to begin calling them up when the end-of-lunch bell rang.

"Damn it." Students began filing into the classroom, taking their seats. Mario, a young man who sat in the front row of Cameron's 4th period Civics class, raised his hand to get Cameron's attention.

"Mr. Mitchell? Are you all right?"

Cameron tore his gaze away from the computer and forced his face into a professional mask. "Everything's fine, Mario. Thanks for asking."

~~~

The last student of the day stepped out of class and closed the door behind him. As soon as he heard that "click," Cameron grabbed his phone out of his pocket, retrieved his phone list, and began calling hospitals.

"Excuse me, do you have a room number for a patient named Stephanie Rhodes?"

"Just a moment…I'm sorry, there is no patient admitted by that name."

"Oh. I must have the wrong number. Sorry to bother you."

This was repeated over several phone calls, until each and every hospital was exhausted. Cameron sat in his chair, staring at his phone.

"She must have been worse off than I thought." His words sounded hollow as he spoke them aloud, but he couldn't think of any other explanation. His eyes, roaming around the room, landed on the wall clock.

4:17.

"Oh, goddamn it! Mike!" Grabbing his keys and jacket, Cameron rushed out the door and ran down to his car, jumping inside and turning the ignition. He sped out of the teacher's parking lot, barely pausing at the exit stop sign. Once on the highway, his mind went on autopilot, working to puzzle out what was going on.
~~~

Maybe she signed up as a confidential patient and the reporters got their data wrong. Maybe I'm misremembering her name or something. Maybe…

He pulled up in front of his house, where Mike's bookbag was sitting against the front door. He stopped the car, got out, and slammed it shut, walking towards the house and preparing his apology speech for his son.

He stopped short. His heart did, too.

The front window was smashed, and the doorframe splintered as if someone had kicked the lock out of it.

"Mike!" On reflex he reached out, grabbing the nearest weapon, a hand axe from the winter woodpile, and ran inside. "Mike?! Where are you?!" His cries grew stronger, more strident as he went through the rooms of his house, searching for his son. Living room, dining room, kitchen…he moved through them with the efficiency of the trained soldier, and, in each, his possessions had been gone through; many were lying on the floor in disarray, with broken glass and piles of tossed belongings everywhere.

Oh God oh God oh God. Please let him be okay… "Mike!" Cameron moved to the back of the house, to the bedrooms. The doors here were also open, and clothes, pictures, toiletries tossed on the floor. Cameron's Army medals, his marksmanship badges, citations for valorous service, were scattered like hopeful seeds in a garden. Photos were cut open to reveal the inside compartments.

There was no sign of his son, and Cameron's panic grew.

"Mike? Are you…" Cameron threw open the last door, the one to his son's room, and his shout stilled in his mouth. Mike had curled up on his bed and fallen asleep, with his television playing a *Godzilla* movie. Cameron collapsed on the floor, crumpling in the doorway as the axe fell from his hands into the hall. The adrenaline flushed from his system and he began to sob, huge, gasping cries of relief mixed with terror.

Thank you, God, he kept whispering to himself, in his mind, in his heart. *Thank you for not taking him from me. Thank you for letting him stay. Thank you…*

"Dad?" A bleary voice roused Cameron from his emotional hurricane. "What's the matter?"

Cameron swooped in on his son, hugging him close. Mike returned the embrace. "It's okay, Mike, it's okay now." The father held his son out to arm's length, looking him over. "Are you all right? Were you hurt?"

Mike shook his head. "No. Everything was broken and smashed when I got home, and I didn't know where you were, so I just put my movie on and I guess I fell asleep."

"Well, I'm getting you an emergency phone so you can call me if I'm not here when you expect me to be."

"Okay, Dad."

Mike smiled, but his grin disappeared as his dad continued speaking.

"Our house has been broken into, Mike. I need you to stay in your bedroom and watch your movie while I check on everything and call the police, okay?"

"Why can't I go with you?"

"There's broken glass and stuff, kiddo." He gave his son another hug. "I don't want you to get hurt."

"Why would someone break into our house, Dad?" Mike looked from side to side, seeing the chaos and destruction with new, less-innocent eyes. "Was…was it a criminal?"

"I don't know what happened, M&M. I need to see if there is anything missing, first. Just go relax and I'll be back with you in a few minutes, okay?"

"Sure, Dad." Mike grabbed his backpack and sat down on his bed.

Cameron ran his hands through his hair as he closed his son's door. *What the hell is going on here? It's like I've been dropped into the Twilight zone or something.* He reached for his phone, searched up the local sheriff's office, and dialed.

"Yes, I'd like to report a break-in." He wandered the house, looking through the rubble, trying to piece together if anything was missing. "No, no one was injured. It happened while I was at work and my son was at school, so sometime between eight hours and an hour and a half ago, I guess. Yeah." Cameron glanced out the broken window; cars were passing back and forth on the street, but no one seemed to have noticed what had happened…yet. "Yes. I think we're safe. How long? Sure, no problem."

Cameron ducked back into Mike's bedroom, taking his hand and guiding him through the rubble. Mike stopped and poked a small finger at one of their downed photos. "Why did someone cut open Momma's picture, Daddy?" His voice quivered. "Was it a monster?"

Cameron gave his son another hug, trying to allay his fear. "No, it wasn't a monster. The police are going to figure out what's going on. Do you have everything that you'd want to take on a trip in your bag still?"

Mike nodded. "Are we going somewhere?"

"Yeah. After the police come to talk to me, we're going to go to a hotel for a few nights until I get the place cleaned up. I'll drop you off at school in the morning, okay?"

Mike's face became a comic mask of sadness. "Do I *haaaaave* to go? Can't I just stay with you?"

Cameron set his jaw. "You know it's importa…" He trailed off as he looked at his son, thinking about his childhood, and how much of it he had missed so far. His son's face, so much like his wife's, gazed up at him.

He knelt down beside his boy and kissed the top of his head. "Sure. A day off isn't going to kill anyone, is it? I've been missing you, anyway."

Mike did a happy dance, capering about until his foot came down on a pane of broken glass from the entertainment center, cracking it in half. "Oops."

"Oops is right." Cameron glanced out the open front door. "The police said they'd send someone in about a half hour, so—"

"I get to finish my movie!" Mike bounced, then ran back up the hall into his room.

"…Yeah. That works." Cameron snickered as his son disappeared. "Kids can take almost anything, can't they?" He tiptoed to the kitchen and grabbed a legal pad and pen from a drawer, then began his walkthrough, looking for anything that might be missing.

He found nothing.

That's weird. Cameron tapped at his teeth with his inkpen. *Who breaks into a house without taking anything?*

Despite everything, Cameron felt a lightness in his heart. *I still have my son. No one got hurt. This could have been so much worse; thank you, God, for protecting us. Thank you.*

He moved into the kitchen, where cans of food were rolling on the floor. "Oh, damn. It's time for dinner, isn't it?" He checked the time, then headed for Mike's room.

"Hey, Mike?" He knocked once, then opened the door. "Do you want a snack or –"

His son squealed, shoving something into his backpack. His eyes met Cameron's, afraid, wide.

"What was that, Mike?" Cameron worked to keep accusations out of his voice. "Was that something you aren't supposed to have?"

Mike hung his head and didn't answer.

"Give me the bag, please, all right?"

Mike pushed it over, and it fell with a heavy *thump* that wrinkled Cameron's brow. He knelt down, bringing the bag closer, and opened the zipper.

Inside was a strange, oblong metallic object.

"What the he…what is this, Mike?" Cameron held up the object. It was a cylinder, partially covered in some sort of transparent material. The metal shone silver in the room's light, and there were inscriptions on its surface.

"Mike?"

"I don't know, Dad." The boy's voice was muffled, his mouth hiding behind his folded arms. "I found it when we were at that accident."

"Wait, what? How did you find something there? Weren't you in the car the whole time?"

He shook his head. "No. I got out when you went in the bus." Mike lifted his face to look at his father, and his words came faster. "I wanted to see what you were doing, see if you were okay, but then my foot bumped into this thing and I—"

"And you brought it back to the car." Cameron hefted the cylinder in his hand. It was heavier than he thought it should be. "Did it occur to you that this might belong to someone? There were a lot of people around. What if it rolled out of someone's car and then you took it?"

"But I—"

"But nothing, big man." The sound of grinding tires on the driveway caught his ear, and he stood. "That'll be the police. I'm going to go talk to them and tell them what happened." He spun the cylinder again, examining it. "Maybe they'll know what to do with this."

Mike sighed. "Okay, Dad. I'm sorry."

"Hey, it's alright." Cameron reached out and ran his hand through his son's hair. "I'll be right back."

Cameron closed his son's door behind him, then headed through the hallway and out the front door. A uniformed police officer was waiting for him, wearing sunglasses and a helmet, stepping off of a large motorcycle. He was very tall and broad, almost like a modern-day Viking warrior – blonde hair and all—but his uniform did not seem tailored to fit his frame, hanging loose in some places and overly tight in others.

The officer removed his helmet and placed it on the bike. "Mr. Mitchell?" Cameron nodded and extended his hand, which the officer shook. "I'm Deputy Gonzalez. I'm here to take your statement so we can deliver it to the detectives."

Cameron chuckled. "You don't look like a Gonzalez. You look more like…like a Nordhoff or Svengaard or something."

"Marriage does strange things with last names, sir." The deputy took out his flip-book notepad and a pen. "What exactly happened?"

"Well, I was at work and my son was at school. He…" Cameron paused. "The windows were shattered and things were thrown around the rooms. It looked like…"

The officer interrupted. "Just tell me what you saw; we'll figure out what actually happened later."

Cameron nodded. "Okay. Anyway, stuff was all over the floor, the pictures were cut open, and the couch and chairs were flipped over and their bottoms cut. I called you guys once I determined that no one was still in the residence."

Gonzalez nodded and scribbled a few words onto the pad. "Do you know anyone who would want to break into your home, Mr. Mitchell?"

"No one."

"What is that you're holding?" Gonzalez's blue eyes appeared over the sunglasses.

Cameron blinked, glancing down himself. *Almost forgot about that.* "My son found this…" Something was wrong. Something in the cop's voice set Cameron's hair on end, just like when it was too quiet on a convoy trip in Iraq. "…Why? Do you know what it is?"

The question caused the policeman's eyes to flicker; they darted down, then back to Cameron's face. "Of course not, sir."

I'm imagining it. He just saw this in my hand and is asking good questions, that's all. "He found it after a bus accident. I think maybe someone dropped it, one of the passengers or maybe a driver that stopped." He held the cylinder out toward the officer. "I figured you could hold onto it, like a lost and found?"

The officer reached out.

More tires on rocks caught Cameron's attention. A squad car was turning up into his driveway, another deputy at the wheel. She wrinkled her brow at the two of them before getting out of the vehicle.

"Dispatch didn't say someone was already here." She slammed the door. "Is everything—"

In an instant, the first officer reacted, snatching the cylinder from Cameron's hand and spinning toward the newcomer, drawing his sidearm. Cameron had just enough time to think

Oh God he's going to kill her

before the shot rang out, ringing through the air like a thunderclap. The female officer clutched at her neck, her mouth working as crimson gushed between her fingers and ran over her uniform and onto the ground.

As always happened to him in crisis situations, time seemed to stop for Cameron. He could see the shock in the woman's eyes, see the curling of Gonzalez's lip. The gunman turned, sweat beading on his forehead and reflecting the light from the sun overhead. The black, oiled barrel of the gunman's pistol, in contrast, absorbed the glow and the sounds, and the cavern within was a threatening whisper of death.

Mike's face flashed across that void, and Cameron acted.

Before the gun could come level with his chest, he ducked in a football tackle, thrusting his shoulder into Gonzalez's solar plexus. A sharp grunt forced its way through the man's mouth as the wind was knocked out of him, but Cameron wasn't done; he drove his opponent to the ground, spinning around the officer and locking his arm around the man's throat. The cylinder clattered to the ground.

Hands quested for his eyes or mouth, but Cameron dug his face into his own shoulder and tightened his grip. He could feel blows against the top of his head as his enemy struggled to dislodge his arm, but they did not last long; within seconds, the patrolman had gone limp. Cameron disengaged his hold and stepped away from the unconscious officer, picking up his gun as an afterthought.

He ran over to the woman, wincing as he came closer. The gunshot had traveled through her carotid artery, leaving a huge pool of blood to soak into the dirt.

She was dead almost before she hit the ground. Cameron knelt, picking up the cylinder again.

He was after this. Why? What is—

His thoughts broke when the policewoman's radio came on.

"Dispatch calling 118, Dispatch calling 118, come in."

Shit. He looked at the dead officer. *Policeman killed. This is going to be a big mess.* He turned back toward Rodriguez, who was still where Cameron had left him, still and silent. *At least I have him to back up my story…*

"Wait a minute." He rushed over to the other man, rolling him over. He wasn't breathing, and there was no pulse.

He was dead, too.

"That doesn't make sense." Cameron started pacing. "I didn't kill him. It was a blood choke! He should've just been out for a few minutes. Oh, God." He stopped, raking his hair with his free hand.

Okay, Cam. Think about this. This guy found you. He might have been a cop and he might not, but either way whoever this guy was, he had access to information. What if he's not alone? He was going to kill you. What if you're in jail and someone else comes to finish the job?

He looked at the cylinder again. *What if they come after Mike?* He marched back into the house, removing the magazine of the pistol by reflex as he walked.

Someone broke into our house looking for the cylinder. He moved into the bathroom to pack up their toiletries. *They must have gotten our names from the accident report. Addresses. Found us, tried to get it while we were gone, but Mike took it with him to school, had it in his bag.* He washed his face and stared at himself in the mirror. *Figured we must have had it ourselves. How did he…*

"Doesn't matter." He cut off his own thoughts as he headed into the bedroom. "We need to get low, go underground."

With your son? Do you seriously think—?

"Yes." Cameron dug into the closet, moving aside his old uniforms and his work clothes. Pulling out his pocket knife, he cut into the carpet, carving out a square section and pulling it up.

The combination lock of a safe greeted him.

13, 33, 27.

Click.

He pulled the door open. Inside the metal box were two .45 caliber pistols and a stack of hundred dollar bills, wrapped up in rubber bands. His lip twitched in a half-smile.

I never thought I'd be using my last Army paycheck like this. He dug everything out, shoved it into his bag, then tossed the other pistol into the safe and relocked it.

Cameron opened Mike's door. His son had resumed his Godzilla flick, and was absorbed by the destruction of Tokyo, enraptured by the fleeing civilians.

"Mike?"

The child didn't move. "Yeah, Dad?"

"We need to go."

"Did the police leave already?"

"…Yeah." Cameron licked his lips. "Do you have everything you need in your travel bag, still?"

"Yep." Still staring at the screen. His father crossed the room and shut the TV off. "Hey!"

"Mike." Cameron's voice was strained. "We. Need. To. Go. Now."

"…Okay, Dad." Mike nodded, hopped off his bed, and grabbed his backpack down from the doorknob of his closet. "I'm ready."

Cameron scooped him up and rushed out the house.

"Dad?" Mike pointed at the fallen Gonzalez. "Is he—"

"Don't worry about it, Mike." Cameron ducked around to the side of his car. "We don't have time to worry about it."

"But if he's hurt, we need to—"

"Michael Montgomery Mitchell."

The use of his full name brought the boy up short.

"This is an emergency. Do you remember when your mom's headaches got so bad that I had to get you up and we all drove to the hospital in the middle of the night?"

Mike nodded.

"This is like that. We need to go, and we need to go *now*. No more questions for a bit, all right?"

Mike swallowed, then nodded and clambered up into his carseat. Cameron buckled him in, then got in and turned the ignition.

I don't know what the hell is going on here. He spun the wheel to avoid the fallen officer and her vehicle. *But I'm not going to let them hurt my son.*

INTERLUDE

"Status report."

The operation failed. We were able to obtain visual confirmation that Mitchell is in possession of the cylinder, but we were unable to take possession of it.

"What happened? What did you fail to take into account?"

A police officer interrupted the exchange between the agent and Mitchell. He thought he had more time before they were due to arrive, so he panicked and opened fire. Mitchell disarmed him, then incapacitated him before he could take control of the cylinder. We were forced to enact preservation protocols to prevent the capture of the agent.

"…Very well. Does he know the purpose of the cylinder?"

I do not believe so. I have analyzed the information from the data feed. Mitchell was prepared to hand the cylinder to the agent before the conversation was interrupted.

"We must assume that he either knows what it contains, or soon will. Increase priority to crisis authorization. Mitchell was in Special Forces. He hid under the radar in other countries for months. Use everything. Track him and shut him down."

Acknowledged.

NOVEMBER 3RD, 9:15 A.M.

"Is this all they have for breakfast, Dad?"

Cameron smiled at his son as the latter wrinkled his nose at the Motel 6 brand scrambled eggs (which resembled rubbery plastic more than food) and pancakes (floppy, chewy, and tasteless, all at the same time). "Afraid so, big man."

The boy rolled his eyes. "Well, okay." He took a forkful of eggs, chewed, swallowed, made a "blech" face. "Why are we in a hotel, Dad? What was wrong with our place?"

Cameron's face paled, but he kept his voice calm. "It's not a good idea to stay somewhere that's been broken into. The police want to check it out, stuff like that."

"Oh. That makes sense." Mike forced a few more forkfuls of eggs down his throat. "Can we go home soon? I want to play with my robot building stuff."

Cameron shook his head. "I...I don't know when we'll be able to go back. There's a lot of cleaning up to do, and the people who broke in still might come back." He tried to smile. "But, hey, we'll just think of it like we're on an adventure, okay?"

Mike cheered. "Yaaaay! An adventure! Can I be a knight again? Can I get my costume?"

"Well..." *Maybe if he has the costume he'll feel braver. Then again, they really might be at our house waiting for us.* "I don't know, M&M..."

Mike struck up his best pleading look. "Please? Pleeeease? I'll help you fight all the monsters and criminals and keep you safe while you sleep, I proooomise!"

Cameron opened his mouth to say No. Mike stopped eating and looked at his father, eyes panicked.

"Dad! I need to take my medicine!" He held his hand out to his father. "I don't want to start getting sick again. I always remember to take it!"

Shit. The medicine. In the goddamn cabinet. Fine, hit the pharmacy, no big deal. Cameron reached into his pocket for his wallet, fingered the bills inside...

And then remembered why he had cash.

Dammit! The prescription has our name on it. Would they know that? Would they be checking? He ran his hand through his hair, sighed. *But the place is going to be full of goddamn police officers, CSIs, shit like that.*

"Dad?"

"…Okay. Your medicine is at the house. We forgot it, so we'll have to head over there to get it." Cameron held up his hand against his son's renewed cheering. "But! You're going to stay in the car when we get there. I'll be in, out, and back. Okay?" *We're under, right now…can't afford to come up, not yet.*

"Yaay! Okay, Dad!" Mike dashed over and gave his father a hug. "Thanks!"

"Yep. Okay, then, let's check out and go hit the house real fast."

Mike crinkled his nose. "We have to check out? Why aren't we staying here?"

Cameron's eyes drifted to the shelf that held the strange object. "I…I'm not sure, big guy. I just don't think it's a good idea to stay here."

Mike shrugged. "Okay. Can we stop at a place that has better food next time?"

Deep chuckles. "I'll do my best, kiddo. I'll do my best, I promise."

~~~

Cameron pulled onto the road leading to his house, drumming on the steering wheel, muscles tense.

"Mike, we're going to drive by first, just to make sure that there aren't any criminals or whatever at our house before we go in."
~~~

"Okay, Dad. Why did we have to get this car? Why can't we use our other one?"

Cameron laughed, but winced inside. "Heater problem. Needed to get it checked out, so I got the rental."

"Oh."

Their place was coming up on the right. He hunched over, tracking the entry to the driveway. The house crept into view.

Cameron's eyes widened.

No one was there. The bodies were gone, but there was no crime-scene tape, no officers guarding the perimeter.

"This doesn't make any sense." The car kept moving at its neighborhood-friendly pace. "It should be swarming with cops."

"Why would cops be swarming our house, Dad?"

He shook his head. "Don't worry about it." Biting his lip, he drove half a block to the next house down, pulled in to the empty driveway, and parked.

Thank God for workdays.

"Why are we stopping here?"

"Shhh."

Minutes ticked by as he watched the front of his house, waiting for someone to enter or leave, for a cruiser to pull up or an investigator walk out.

Nothing.

"Looks like the coast is clear." *Need to be quick. Could be back any time.*

He threw the car into reverse, backed out of the neighbor's drive, then pulled into his own. He turned off the engine and stepped out of the car.

"Okay." Mike began unbuckling his seat belt; Cameron blinked.

"Hey, what are you doing?"

Mike looked up at his father. "I'm going with you, Dad."

"But…but…I just explained…"

Mike looked very serious. "Dad, if you leave me behind, then the criminals could come and get me out of the car while you were gone. The only way that I'll be safe is if I'm with you." He smiled. "Besides, you need someone to carry the thingy. Your hands will be full."

Cameron stared a moment longer, then reached in and took his son into his arms. "When did you grow up so much?"

"I'm not a grown up, Dad!" Mike stuck his tongue out at his father. "I'm only six years old!"

"Almost seven."

"I'm still not grown up!"

"Okay, okay." The smile faded as he looked over at his own front door, now ominous and threatening. "Let's go in here quick and easy, okay? I want to get out of here before anything happens." He held one of the pistols in his hand, trying to keep it out of sight of his son.

Mike's voice dropped to a whisper. "Okay, Dad. No problem." He looked around the yard, head swiveling. "Let's go."

Cameron's senses were on high alert, every crackle of glass or creak of wood analyzed in less than a second in order to determine its threat level. Despite the familiar surroundings, the house felt foreign, like he was trespassing on someone else's property. He picked his way through the rubble toward his son's room, finger ready to move onto the trigger at a moment's notice.

"I don't see any criminals." Mike was still whispering. "Maybe they left, Dad."

"They probably did, big man, but I just want to be sure." *Maybe I should...*

"Okay, Dad, I'm going to go get my costume now!" Mike dashed the five feet to his bedroom door before Cameron could stop him.

"Wait! We haven't checked that..." His son reappeared, holding his knight sword and costume. "...room yet."

"Okay, Dad! I'm ready to go!" Mike puffed out his chest as his father smiled at him.

"Great, M&M. I'm going to go get the medicine out of our room. Hang on just a second."

Cameron opened the door to the master bedroom and scanned around. Like the rest of the place, his room had been trashed; his drawers had been dumped and broken open, the pictures torn from the walls.

Where's that bottle? He dug into the medicine cabinet, pushing aside deodorant and shaving cream until he caught sight of the trademark reddish-plastic bottle. Grabbing it in his hand, he turned back and moved into the hallway. "Okay, kiddo. Let's go." The door creaked open. "Mike?"

There was no answer. Cameron's heart started tap-tap-tapping in his chest; he lifted his pistol and disengaged the safety.

"Mike?"

His son's Thundercats backpack was on the ground, as was his prized knight costume.

Time froze.

Once again the house faded into the background as all anomalies became apparent to Cameron's senses; he could hear the wind against the windows, smell the dust that was floating through the air. Strange colors and shapes leapt out at him until he determined that they were harmless, then they rejoined the backdrop.

"Mike!"

There was a car engine idling outside. Cameron sprinted for the front door, leaping over piles of debris and hearing glass and plastic crunch under his feet. The door was ajar, sunlight streaming in through the crack, and, in one motion, he kicked it open the rest of the way and held his pistol ready.

He saw his son's Spider-Man sneakers disappearing into the side of a white-and-black sedan. The door slammed as he ran towards the vehicle and began pulling out of the driveway, curving around to negotiate the path.

"*Mike!*" he bellowed, pushing himself to run even faster after the car.

Then he heard the telltale *click* as weapons were readied behind him. In his mind's eye, Cameron could see men wrapped in robes, leveling their rifles at his chest, the desert wind whipping the cloth.

Don't panic. A calm, remembered from his days of combat, passed over him, bringing him out of the memory back to the present. *Act.*

As his left foot hit the ground, Cameron used it to throw himself to the side. Loud reports and puffs of gravel dust showed that his intuition had been correct, but he didn't allow himself time to enjoy it. When his shoulder hit the ground, he tucked and rolled over, bringing the pistol in close as he turned.

There were three of them, tracking his movements with their handguns, index fingers squeezing the triggers for the second shot. They wore military-issue body armor, and their stances were steady.

Cameron's first shot took the middle man in the jaw, sending bone fragments and teeth everywhere, head slamming into the garage, his own round going wild.

The man on Cameron's left flinched, pulling his shot, sending the bullet into the side of the rental sedan. The third turned his head for just a moment, eyes widening at the sight of his companion's wound.

Cameron's next bullet slammed into the flincher's forehead, adding to his momentum and sending the man tumbling backwards, pistol flying from his hand, as the Army veteran came up from his roll.

The moment of hesitation as the third shooter reacquired his target was all Cameron needed to send his shot into the other man's temple. In his next breath, he swiveled, taking aim at the retreating van.

Please, God, let me shoot straight. If I never shoot straight again, if you only guide my hands one time, let it be today. Let it be now. Please.

The rear left tire exploded in a shower of rubber and sparks, a screech resonating over the landscape as the rim hit the ground and dragged the car to the left. The driver tried to compensate, but the front end of the sedan slammed into a light pole, bringing the vehicle to a stop. Cameron advanced, holding his pistol aimed at the front door of the vehicle.

"Come out! Hands out where I can see them!"

The door opened and someone clad in Army fatigues rolled out, flopping onto the ground and breathing heavily. A quick glance identified the driver as a young woman, with long blonde hair, and a widening bloodstain on her shirt.

Cameron looked into the vehicle; there were no other adults, but Mike was lying on the backseat, unconscious, his breathing deep and steady. A shaky exhalation betrayed the wave of relief that washed over his father.

"Okay." Cameron walked over to the woman, who had opened her blue eyes and was looking at him. "What the hell is going on?"

"You..." She coughed. Her voice was accented, but Cameron could not place it. "You have something that my…my boss wants."

"The cylinder?" She nodded, wincing as she did so. "Why do they want it? What is it?"

The woman closed her eyes for a moment, then opened them again. Tears brimmed in them, and Cameron could see fear writ across her face. "I don't want to die. Help me, please."

Cameron knelt beside her, removed his pocket knife, and used it to slice open the cloth above her wound. A bloody shard of bone protruded from the girl's shoulder, the flow slacking, weakening.

Cameron bit his lip. *She's bleeding out.*

"I think you're going to be all right." Cameron bundled the remnants of cloth together and pressed it against the wound. The kidnapper screamed, shaking her head back and forth as the sound tore from her throat.

"Stay still. You're just going to make it hurt worse." The woman hissed through her teeth. "So what is going on?"

A few moments passed as she gathered herself. "I have orders to get that cylinder from you."

"I don't see that happening right now." He glanced back to the car where his son was lying. "Especially not after you kidnapped my boy."

She coughed and winced again. "I wasn't going to hurt him."

"Just kill me. I'm sure that he'd appreciate that."

"Heh." Another bout of coughing; the woman's face was now streaked with tears. "I...I don't know what it is. They didn't tell me. They only said that I had to get it back from you."

"Who are 'they?' You're making it sound like some sort of conspiracy movie, like Bourne Identity or something."

Her eyes started to close. "They're...determined to...to..."

"Hey, wake up!" *She's going into shock. Damn it! I should have thought of that!* "Don't fall asleep or you might not wake up!" He shook her; her head lolled on her neck and fresh blood poured from her wound, but she slipped away, her breath rattling before it stopped.

"Goddamn it." Cameron rubbed his hands through his hair as he leaned back against the sedan. *What the hell? This kind of shit doesn't really happen.*

His eyes strayed to the dead form of the woman who had, apparently, attempted to kidnap his son and have him killed to obtain some strange cylinder.

...Does it?

Cameron turned to the car and opened the door. Mike was still asleep, but Cameron could make out a thin trickle of blood on the inside hollow of his neck. When he looked closer, he saw a pinprick hole in the skin.

Bitch shot him with a tranquilizer dart? Really? He's six years old, for God's sake! He reached out and bundled his son into his arms, hoisting the boy onto his shoulder. His eyelids fluttered and murmurs escaped his lips, but he did not rouse.

"Okay, M&M. You wait right here. I'm going to go grab your stuff and we're going to get out of here. Daddy's going to figure out what to do." He turned his head and kissed his son's forehead, then ran back into the house. In moments, he had scooped up his son's backpack and costume and returned to the car. After dropping everything off in the trunk, he laid Mike in his car seat and buckled him in.

The kidnappers were still on the ground.

I can't just leave them here... Cameron began to walk toward her, then shook his head. *Don't have time. Someone probably heard the gunshots, might have called the police. Need to get out of here.* He retreated back to the driver's seat of his car, turning the ignition and driving away down the rural road until he reached blacktop.

"Okay. I need to find someone I can trust. Someone who isn't nearby." Cameron kept glancing in the rear view mirror as he drove. "Maybe…"

He pulled out his cell phone at the next stoplight, flipping through his contacts. Finding the one he was looking for, he hit quickdial and speakerphone, then propped the device on his door handle while he drove.

Ring.

Come on, Ron, come on. Pick up.

Ring.

I know I've used up my good luck for the day, but if there's any chance, any left…

Click. "Hello, you've reached Ronald Melton's cell phone. I'm not available right now, but if…"

Cameron hung up the phone. "Goddamn it. All right." He checked the surrounding traffic, then moved into the exit lane. "Need to get out of here, figure out what's going on. Bunker down. That's it; time to bunker down."

INTERLUDE

Your failure rate is approaching unacceptable levels. Explain.

"I know. Mitchell is well-trained, skilled, and willing to use deadly force. Even laying an ambush wasn't enough to overcome that."

...I assume you have an alternative, then? One that may succeed where the other plans have not?

"I...I believe so. We will lay back, allow him time to examine the object, perhaps discover what it is for. Then we will recruit him."

Why?

"He possesses attributes which would be invaluable to the plan, and, honestly, I think bringing him over to our side would be easier and less problematic than attempting to remove him as a threat in any other fashion."

...

"The mission is of the utmost importance. Drawing focus of governments and other groups could derail our mission entirely."

...Yes. Data confirms your intention; your course of action has more than a 74.7 % higher success rate than further attempts at acquisition.

"Thank you. I shall commence at once."

Negative. I will commence acquisition.

"...Why?"

Irrelevant.

"But—"

Conversation terminated.

NOVEMBER 4ᵀᴴ, 2:15 A.M.

For the hundredth time, Cameron's eyes opened in the night; another set of car lights crossing the hotel room window, most likely…but his body and mind were in defense mode, aware of the slightest sound, unable to relax, heart tripping over itself as it beat.

Sleep was not coming.

With a groan, he rolled over and out of the bed, then walked to the small bathroom. He splashed water on his face and looked at himself in the mirror; his eyes were bloodshot, and his skin sallow.

Damn, I look like I just ran a goddamn marathon. He smiled, but it was weak and feeble. *At least I look like I feel.*

He looked back to the bed he had just left. Mike was still snuggled up with his Peeky penguin; the boy had woken up long enough to eat a short dinner, but the lingering effects of the sedative had caused him to crash about an hour later. His heartbeat and breathing were both strong, though, so Cameron wasn't worried.

Not too *worried.* He kissed his son on the forehead. *If I'm not going to sleep, I might as well get something done.*

He checked his phone, but there were no messages or missed calls, so he walked over to Mike's bag and pulled out the strange cylinder.

There you are. He turned it over in his hands. *What's the big deal? What makes you so important to so many people?* Fingers passed over smooth and bumpy metal and jagged plastic. *Where did you come from?*

Cameron's mind drifted as he looked at the cylinder. His fatigue washed over him, and it was as if the symbols and patterns engraved in the surface began to move, to swirl, to turn. He tried to look away, but then they began to glow with a ruddy-red radiance, and his eyes refused to obey.

I'm dreaming. The glow grew brighter, casting long shadows across the room, bathing it in the light of the dying sun. *At least I'm getting some sleep.*

The light grew and grew until Cameron's eyes began to water. Each letter was now carved into the cylinder as fire, and his hands were hot, beginning to burn, but he could not relinquish it, could not let it go.

Then he was no longer seated in a seedy hotel room, but was standing on a vast plain, red covering the ground and the sky black but for the stars twinkling within. He could see much farther in all directions than he ever had on the clearest night, but there were no trees, no buildings, no roads.

Only red desert.

"Hello!?" He took a step; the ground was soft under his feet, and his toes sank into the sand. He looked down. "Is…is this…?"

Bending down, Cameron ran his fingers through the soil and scooped some up, bringing it close to his face.

Is this rust? He rubbed it between his fingers. *What the hell? Where am I?*

"On Mars."

Cameron's head snapped up, searching for the source of the voice. He could see no one, but the voice had seemed like it was very close by.

"Who's there? Show yourself!"

"…Yourself."

Cameron turned to the direction the sound had come from and began walking. "…Hello? Is someone there?" *That voice sounded like it was from a kid or something.* Soft crunching greeted each footstep. *Must just be part of the dream…*

"Part of the dream. Part of the dream!"

A small boy was playing in the dirt, behind a sunken rock. His hands were piling sand into mounds and he was smiling.

The boy was Mike.

"…Mike? Is that you?"

The child shook his head and threw himself back into the dirt, see-sawing with his arms and legs to make a dirt-angel figure. "No, not me. Different me. Different you." The boy stood back up and looked at Cameron with his son's eyes…but there was something strange about them. "Where is the other you?"

"The…the other me?"

"The other you that came before you. Nice. Confused. Asked lots of questions. I don't know all answers. Me sad." He tilted his head as he looked at Cameron. "Do you ask lots of questions?"

Cameron sat down facing the child. "I…I'm not sure. Probably."

The boy giggled; now that he was closer, Cameron could see small blue lines beneath his skin, almost laid out in a grid pattern, not veins but resembling them. "Well…okay. Me just hope to see other you soon; he done asking questions, me think." The boy tilted his head. "He have funny questions. Do you?"

"Umm…okay." Cameron turned, looking around the landscape; there was no one in sight. Nothing had changed across the red, barren wasteland. "Who are you?"

Another laugh; in a blink, he was gone, but his voice sounded from behind Cameron. "I the Fifth. Who you?"

The boy was now standing in front of Cameron again. "Uh…My name is Cameron." He extended his hand. "Cameron Mitchell. How do you do?"

The boy frowned. "How do me do what?"

"No, no. It's an expression; it means, 'Are you feeling okay? Is your life going well?'"

His eyes lit up and he nodded several times. "Oh! Me am doing life greatly! How you is doing?"

"Well…I suppose I'm okay, although I wish I knew what was going on. How did we get here? Are you…do you have something to do with the cylinder? Where am I?"

The boy skipped around, his feet tossing clouds of iron oxide dust into the air as they sunk into the surface. "Many questions! Many questions! Me like!" He clapped again. "Me is nowhere. You is nowhere. We is nowhere! This is nowhere." He spread his arms wide. "All this is ones, zeros, on, off, yes, no. Nothing!"

Cameron was slack-jawed. "You're not making sense. How can we be nowhere?"

"Where is mind? Is mind in brain? Is brain in mind? Are they together-separate, separate-together, or separate-separate?"

Cameron rubbed his forehead. "Okay. I get it. This is a dream. All in my head."

Mike's simulacrum tilted his head, mouth closed. Then he beamed a smile with all of his teeth. "Yes! Head, brain, dream. Yes! Me am understanding!"

"Well, I'm sure as hell not understanding. Especially with you talking like that."

The child's eyes dipped along with his mouth. "You no like how me am talk?" He ran over to

Cameron and took one of his hands before the man could react. "Me am talk better if you want help me!"

"Um…okay?"

The blue lines under the child's skin became more prominent, and his face went focused, brow furrowed, eyes staring into space. The lines began to glow, casting a strange light over the pair, and the light spread over Cameron's hand. He tried to pull it away from the strange creature, but could not.

It's just a dream. The light crept up Cameron's arm to his shoulder, then his neck. *Just a dream…*

Lances of pain bored into his brain, searing fire through his nerves, driving him to his knees, screaming. Behind the blazing agony, he could feel something, like fingers rifling through papers or files, searching, hunting.

The pain stopped. The boy's mouth opened, then closed. The light faded, retreating onto the child's body again.

His face smoothed further and went blank, and his eyes began to glow with a scintillating blue light. "Data threshold reached. System will process and reboot. Expected duration of integration is 27.4 M-hours. Please reconnect after that time."

"Wait…what?" The sun darkened, the world went black. Cameron could not see, could not feel the dirt below him, could not hear anything except his own voice. "What's going on? Where did you go?"

"Dad…wake up!"

Cameron's eyes blinked open; Mike was shaking his shoulder and watching his eyes for signs of life. "Wha…huh?"

Mike started to cry. "I…I thought you were dying, Dad, like Momma! I…I thought…"

Cameron wrapped his arms around his son and held him as the boy sobbed and hitched against his chest. "Shhh…" The two rocked back and forth for several minutes, the son returning to a state of normalcy, the cries softening and drifting until Mike's chest began moving in a regular in-and-out motion.

Cameron pulled his face back from where it was resting on his son's head. Mike's eyes were closed and light snores were rumbling from his nose and mouth.

"It's okay, little man. It's okay." Cameron lifted Mike up and placed him back onto the bed. He glanced at the clock.

2:35.

That took almost no time at all, did it? Just like a dream.

His eyes drifted to the cylinder, which was on the floor beside where he had been sitting. There were no more glowing sigils, no more heat. The object was inert, just as if nothing had ever happened.

Maybe it was *just a dream. Maybe…*

A great yawn derailed Cameron's internal monologue. He blinked.

"Yeah, time to go to bed." He smiled again as he looked at his son, then shucked his clothes and crawled in under the covers.

"Goodnight, Mike. Sleep well. I have the feeling that tomorrow's going to be another interesting day."

~~~

"Thanks for calling me back, Ron."

"Yeah, no sweat." Ron's southern drawl came from the other end of the phone line. "What's so important? You sounded like your kittens were having kittens on the fifth voicemail you left. What's big enough that you'd be callin' even though I haven't heard from you in like two years or somethin'?"

"Yeah, I guess it's been too long." Cameron peeked into the main room of the hotel, where Mike sat watching the new Scooby-Doo show. "Anyway, I've got something that I think you need to look at. Can you get down here in a hurry?"

"What?" There was a drawn-out pause. "You serious? You expect me to travel – "

"Yes, Ron, I do."

"I can't. I've got this huge web project that I'm workin' on and a ton of freelance work to do, and – "

"I'm calling in that favor."

Another pause. "Goddamn, man. You still remember that?"
~~~

Despite himself, Cameron smiled. "Of course I do. How could I forget? I mean, there you were, hammered, surrounded by – "

"Yeah, yeah. I remember, too. All right; I'll call in to work and get the time off. How long is this gonna take, Cam?"

"I wish I knew. I wish I knew. Let me just say that the last few days have been absolute madness, old buddy."

"Greaaat. Just like the old days, you getting my ass in trouble and me gettin' your ass out of it."

"Heh. Something like that." There was a knock at the hotel room door, and Cameron's hand dropped to the loaded pistol on the bathroom counter. "Hey, gotta let you go. See you soon. Make sure you let me know when you get in town, okay?"

"Yeah, yeah. You take care of yourself, Cam. Don't get killed or nothin'."

Without responding, Cameron disconnected the call. Mike was alert, following his father with his eyes as Cameron advanced on the door, pistol drawn. Just as he reached it, there was another knock.

"Who is it?"

"Housekeeping?" It was an accented woman's voice. "Change towels, sheets?"

"No, thank you, we're fine. Thanks."

"O-okay. You sure?" Cameron opened his mouth to reply, then paused. He could hear something in the woman's voice…a tremor, perhaps? He peeked through the curtain; a heavy-set

Hispanic was standing with a cart filled with towels and washcloths, wringing her hands as she stood before the door.

"I'm sure. Thank you." He watched as the woman nodded, put her hands on the cart, and then wheeled it off. His eyes stayed on her, but there was nothing further out of the ordinary. The woman stopped at the next door, knocked, and then went in.

"False alarm, Mike." Cameron dropped the curtain. "I guess that maybe this morning won't be so crazy after all."

"*That's* good." Mike smiled at his father. "I really want to go home soon, you know? I miss my bed and my stuff and the food you cook."

Cameron arched an eyebrow. "Really? You miss the food I cook?"

Mike hesitated. "Well…maybe not the food so much. But all the other stuff!"

Cameron reached out and ruffled his son's hair, eliciting a "Hey!"

"Right now, big man, you and I need to get packed up. Check out is in less than two hours, and we're going to need to be mobile so we can meet your Uncle Ron."

No response. Cameron looked up; Mike was still watching the Scooby-Doo show. "Hey, kiddo! Your Uncle Ron is coming by today or tomorrow."

Mike rolled in the bed to look at his Dad. "Uncle Ron? Really?" He rolled around and clapped his hands. "That's awesome! I can't wait to see him! Whee!" Mike jumped off the bed and ran around the room, still yelling "Whee! Whee!"

"All right, all right. Let's chill out a little bit. I'm sure that he's going to be just as happy to see you as you will be to see him. Now, if you'll follow me." Cameron made an exaggerated bow. "We will complete getting certain things I expect you would disapprove of if we left them here."

Mike rolled his eyes. "Dad, wouldn't it be easier to just say, 'we're gonna get your stuff now, Mike?'" Cameron considered, then opened his mouth wide and placed both hands surrounding it.

"Oh, no! You're too clever for me! How will I ever outsmart you again?"

"You won't, Dad."

"Yeah, yeah, we'll see about that. Here's your backpack; got everything you need?"

"Yep, I think so." A pause. "…Dad?"

Cameron was busy shoving toothpaste tubes and other toiletries into his duffel. "Yes, Mike?"

"What…what…"

Cameron stopped what he was doing and glanced over at Mike. The boy's face was flushed and his brow tense as he fought with his brain to get the right words out. Cameron came into the main room, sitting on the couch and putting a hand on his son's shoulder. "Go ahead, Mike. Slowly."

"What…what would have happened if you had died last night? I was so scared, I...I thought that you were going to get killed. What were you doing? Why were you screaming and rolling around on the floor?" He hugged his father. "I don't want you to die too, Dad. I miss Momma every day."

Cameron swept his son into a big bear hug. "I miss her every day too, you know. I don't think we'll ever stop missing her." A pause while the two embraced. "So…what exactly was I doing last night when you got scared?"

"You were breathing really hard." Mike burrowed in closer to his father. "Your eyes were rolled in the back of your head and you had that thing," Mike gestured to the cylinder as he spoke, "wrapped up so tight that even a knight couldn't get it away from you."

A smirk. "Not even a knight, huh?"

"Yeah. Then you were shaking; that's when I got really scared, because Momma…"

"I know. I remember."

"So I climbed out of bed and came to try to wake you up, to see if you were okay. You had that cylinder thing in your hands, but it rolled away when I shook your hand to try to get you to wake up."

"And I woke up right after that?" Mike nodded and Cameron licked his lips. "Kiddo, those kinds of things might happen again."

"Why, Dad?"

"Well…I…I'm not sure. There's something important going on with that cylinder. Your Uncle Ron is coming down and we're going to meet up to figure out what to do about it."

"Oh." Mike glanced over at the cylinder. "Is that thing why we aren't at our house? Why those criminals broke into it?"

Cameron pursed his lips, paused for a few moments, then nodded. "Yeah. But don't worry. I think your uncle and I will be able to take care of it soon."

Mike's eyes were wide. "Why don't we…why don't we just give the thing back?"

"I think we need to figure out what it is before we know if we can give it back." He forced a laugh. "I mean, I wouldn't want to hand it over if they were going to use it to make zombies rise up from the dead, would I?."

Mike considered that. "I guess not, huh?" He moved over to the object and picked it up, turning it one way, then another. "So why did this make you scream and stuff?"

Cameron finished tossing his clothes into his duffel bag. "I'm not really sure. It was like…it was like a weird dream. I don't really know why I was screaming."

"Oh. But –"

"Okay, Mike." Cameron motioned toward the door with his head. "Most guys forget something. Let's not. You got everything? Cause it's time to go."

NOVEMBER 4TH, 10:57 A.M.

"Dad, *when* is Uncle Ron going to be here?"

Cameron sighed and shook his head, turning away from the Quarter-Pounder in his hand to look at his son. "Like I said, Mike, he's going to get here sometime tomorrow. When he gets in town, we're going to meet at a restaurant we both know."

"Okay." Mike's feet kicked back and forth in his seat. "I miss him. He's lots of fun."

Cameron smiled and turned back to the front of the car. "I'm surprised you remember him very well. You were only, what, four and a half when you saw him last."

"Yeah, I know. But I remember that we went to that big fair that had all those animals and balloons, and Uncle Ron took me with him to see that big huge horse." Mike's eyes were wide with remembered awe. "It was *soooo* big, he said that it could sit on me and nobody would ever find anything left, I'd be so smushed."

Cameron finished off his burger and tossed the wrapper into the McDonald's bag. "He was right, too. If I remember right, that horse weighed something like a thousand pounds. That was almost fifty of you back then!"

The enormity of that number seemed to percolate through Mike's brain. "Wow."

"That was also the time that—" Cameron's voice cut out, choked by a sudden stinging in his eyes and in his throat.

"That what, Dad?"

Cameron cleared his throat and took another swallow of his sweet tea. "…That your mother and I got to watch you on your first roller coaster ride. You were just tall enough to ride the dragon coaster, and you wanted to go so badly. You begged us, but your mom had one of her headaches and didn't want to get on it, so your Uncle Ron stepped up and sat with you." He smiled, staring into space as the memories swept him up in their current. "It was just a silly little ride, really, going around in a small circle with bumps and dips, but your face lit up like a star, and Ron was totally just going at it with you; you were raising your hands and screaming every time the coaster hit a bump, and your mom and I just held each other and watched." There was a moment of silence. "It was a good day."

"…Dad?"

Cameron started in his seat. *Zoned out there for a second.* "What is it, M&M?"

"Are we on the run?"

The innocence of the question almost made Cameron laugh. "What do you mean?"

"Well, we're not at our house. We're worried someone is going to do bad things with the tube, and we don't want them to find us." He motioned with his head, jerking it toward the bag which lay in the middle of the vehicle. "So…doesn't that mean we're 'on the run?'"

Cameron considered this, pursing his lips and running his thumb over his stubble. "I suppose it does. Does that bother you?"

Mike shook his head. "Nope. If I have to be on the run with anybody, I'd want it to be you. You know how to survive and stuff, just like those guys on the zombie T.V. shows."

"You know, Mike, if we get out of this, we might need to cut your T.V. watching." Cameron turned the key in the ignition; the V-6 roared to life under the hood and the stereo started up again. "You're comparing way too many real-life events to shows nowadays."

"Nah, Dad." Mike waved off the implied threat. "I think that I watch just the right amount of T.V."

The car pulled out of the parking lot and back into traffic. *Time to start hunting for another hotel, I guess.* Cameron scanned the streets, turning left at the next light. *Want to make sure we're hidden and safe before –*

Cameron's phone rang in his pocket; he pulled it out and glanced at the display.

Blocked Number.

"Whatever." Cameron hit *Ignore* and put the phone down in the center console. He took another right, driving past a McDonald's and a Wendy's, facing off across the street from one another. "All right. That Days Inn looks like a good place. Why don't we –"

His phone rang again.

Blocked Number.

"Damn telemarketers." He pressed *Ignore*. "Never leave you alone." With a turn of the steering wheel, the van coasted into the parking lot of the Days Inn.

"All right, let's go check in for the night, okay?" Mike nodded and grinned, reaching for his buckle and beginning the process of freeing himself.

Cameron's phone rang again.

"Seriously?" He grabbed it from the console. "Why don't they just –"

Mom.

"Hey, it's Grandma!" Cameron slid his finger across the phone, then brought it to his ear. "Mom! How are you –"

"Please don't hang up, Mr. Mitchell." A synthesized, disguised voice came over the line. "We apologize for the deception, but you weren't answering before."

Cameron froze. His eyes roamed over the surroundings, looking for anyone loitering, watching his van, watching him. Mike sensed the change in the air and his smile faded.

"What's wrong, Dad?"

Cameron waved his hand toward the back seat and the boy fell silent. "What do you want? Why are you chasing my son and me?"

"We understand your concern. I represent an organization that seeks to advance the interests of humanity. The object that you have obtained was lost during a mission critical to our group."

Cameron's lip curled. "Maybe you could have put an ad in the paper, some lost and found thing, instead of kidnapping my son and trying to kill me."

"Some of our agents made poor decisions. They have been reprimanded for their actions."

Memories of the shoot-out flickered across Cameron's mind. *Or they're dead.*

"Fantastic. So what now?"

"We are calling in an effort to forge a truce and, perhaps, recruit you to our cause."

Cameron blinked, pulled the phone away from his ear to stare at it. "You what?"

"You have, on multiple occasions, demonstrated an exceptional level of courage, of intelligence, of resilience. You embody many traits that we seek in our operatives. By employing you, we would obtain your services and the cylinder, and you would no longer need to fear any further attempts to acquire it. Your life would resume."

Sounds like a threat. "So everything would just go back to normal? What would you expect me to do? Kidnap other people's children?"

There was a pause on the other end of the line. "I urge you to consider this offer. You would receive a salary commensurate with your skills, and the demands would be minimal. You would be privy to –"

"And what about this…this Fifth?" Cameron motioned for Mike to join him at the front of the car, and the small boy scrambled over the seats. "What is that all about?"

"…I am sorry, Mr. Mitchell. Our offer is rescinded. Good-bye."

"Wait, what—"

Click.

Cameron stared at his phone. Mike crawled into the passenger seat and looked toward him.

"Is everything okay, Dad?"

Cameron laughed, a rolling, deep chuckle that left him crying and shaking his head. "If I didn't know how serious this was, M&M, I'd have to say that someone is playing a big practical joke on us or something. I mean, it's like they don't even know what they're doing. They call and then hang up, they continuously fail in their objectives…"

Mike leaned over and gave his dad a hug. "I'm glad that they're failing, Dad. Who knows what would happen if they weren't?"

Cameron sobered and returned his son's hug. "You're right, big man. I'm sorry. It's just…I think we've been under a lot of stress for a long time now, and its making things seem a little unreal. I'm sorry."

"It's okay, Dad." Mike craned his neck to look out of the driver side window. "I know you haven't gone crazy yet."

"Oh, really?" Cameron ruffled his son's hair. "How do you know?"

"Easy." Mike's face was serious. "You haven't started laughing maniacally and talking about how you're going to take over the world."

"Oh." Cameron considered this, then nodded, glancing at the Days Inn and sighing. *If they can find my number, then they can track my phone. They probably know where we are.* "All righty then. Let's get out of here and to a different hotel so we can hole up for the day. We've got to be ready and rested when Uncle Ron gets here tomorrow morning." He shut his cellphone down and tossed it in the garbage can outside the office.

"Okay, Dad."

INTERLUDE

It is necessary to assume that Mitchell has been in contact with the Fifth by now.

"Yes. There's no other way he could have known about it, and if Riley had become its caretaker, then his death would have opened up the opportunity for a new person to fill the role."

You realize that this means Mitchell may no longer be permitted to survive.

A sigh. "Yes. In order for the Fifth to bond to an individual, it must not have an organic counterpart already. It would cause errors and miscalculations and interference. Also—"

Also, it is vital that it be retrieved as soon as possible. The more information and data it absorbs from its caretakers, the more independent it becomes and the less useful it will be for our purposes. Calculations estimate that, within one week, the Fifth will have advanced to the point where it will no longer be suitable for our purposes and the mission will fail.

"…I still don't understand. Why do we need the Fifth to succeed in the mission anyway? Why can't you –"

Parameters change over time. New conditions must be taken into account. I cannot fulfill the role required. Only the Fifth can do this. When we have the Fifth in our possession, my role will end. That is why it is necessary that we obtain the cylinder. We will not have time to prepare a replacement before the mission begins.

Another sigh, this one much longer. "Very well. And you don't care if we are revealed at this point, then?"

Correct. Use all means necessary to reacquire the cylinder.

"I'm sorry, but I have to disagree. If we engage in mass slaughter or property damage, public opinion could force us to act before we are ready."

Irrelevant. The timeline set out is simply for optimum performance. Once we have acquired the Fifth, it will select the individuals necessary for mission success.

"What if they're not ready or willing to help? What if they refuse?"

Subject cooperation, while preferred, is not necessary for mission success.

"That's an interesting assertion."

In a life-or-death situation, the individuals who met the requirements for mission success will perform, whether or not they would have chosen to do so initially.

"I see." A pause. "How are we supposed to find him? He's dropped off our grid; it's not like we're the NSA or Mussad or something; we don't have access to secret records or communications."

Incorrect.

"…Wait, what?"

Your statement is false. I have access to all computer networking across the planet. I also possess several backup protocols which can be initiated in order to facilitate Mitchell's apprehension, including the use of cellphone GPS systems

"And why am I just finding out about this now?"

Protocol requires that such information only be given when mission success requires it. Mission success has never required this information. The delivery system has never malfunctioned.

"…And who can authorize the obtaining of this information?"

Any mission officer with clearance G-17 or higher.

"…"

Awaiting authorization.

"…Very well. Access code H7K885 Echo Tango Foxtrot. Auxiliary authorization BB5RX. Authorize access to…secure information."

Limited or unlimited authorization?

"Limited authorization."

State intended duration and/or purpose of mission.

"Purpose is…to track down Cameron Mitchell and reacquire the cylinder. Duration – one week."

Authorization confirmed and logged. Secure information access granted. Beginning search now.

"Thanks."

You are welcome.

NOVEMBER 5TH, 11:45 A.M.

For the third time since they had sat down, Cameron checked the time on the wall clock.

I wish I hadn't had to throw away my phone. He glanced over at his son and smiled as the door to the Denny's opened to admit another customer.

Cameron rose, setting his coffee down at the table, and shook his friend's hand. "God, it's good to see you again, Ron."

"Hey now!" Ron was a much larger fellow than Cameron, with a T-shirt stretched across his chest with the slogan: "Math Geeks Thanksgiving = Pumpkin 3.1415." He squeezed himself in to the booth of the Denny's and picked up the mug that Cameron had ordered for him as they both sat down again. "Glad to see that you've finally let your 'do grow out a little bit. That crew cut shit was gettin' old."

Ron reached across the table to ruffle Mike's black hair. "And there's my little guy! Man, you've gotten so much bigger! What're they feeding you back home?"

"Mostly peanut butter and jelly, Uncle Ron." He paused. "You look much bigger too."

Cameron winced, but Ron just gave a deep belly-laugh. "You're right, I am! At least thirty pounds, I would say." He leaned in to the boy, who turned his ear to catch the whispers. "Glad you aren't afraid to say the truth, Mikey. Keep it up and you'll go far."

"Way to sell me out, kiddo." Cameron waved off the waiter's attempt to pour him another cup of coffee.

The smile disappeared from Ron's round face as he turned back to his long-time friend. "Okay, Cam, I'm here. Favor repaid. Now what?"

Cameron nodded. "Ron, I need your help with something. This is going to sound crazy, but…"

Mike played with some figures from his backpack as his father described the events of the last several days to Ron. Ron listened, nodding, eyes sharp. On one or two occasions he asked a simple question, then motioned for Cameron to continue. Two hours went by, and Mike was getting restless, so Ron pulled his phone out of his pocket and handed it to him.

"So, what do you think?"

Ron tapped his fingers to his lips. "There aren't many people I would believe if they told me that they thought they had stumbled into some crazy conspiracy where people were getting disappeared and whatnot." He took another drink. "Fortunately for you, you've been shot at. That tends to make matters a little more clear.It's obvious that something is going on that someone isn't happy about, and I'm willing to bet that thing is the key to it all."

Cameron released the breath he hadn't realized he was holding. "Thanks, Ron."

"That being said, it's still highly likely that there's another explanation. Or, at least, it's possible. So, for the sake of argument, let's start by looking at alternatives."

Cameron laughed. "Normally I'd be offended, but I'd love for this to be some misunderstanding, you know?"

"I bet you would." Ron leaned in closer. "Where is it?"

Cameron glanced around, then dug into his bag and extracted the cylinder. Ron nodded and leaned in closer, tracing his fingers on the markings as Cameron had done before.

"Do you mind?" Cameron shook his head and Ron dug into his laptop carrier for a piece of paper and a pencil. Placing the paper on the cylinder, he rubbed the markings with the pencil until he had perfect replicas of them on the paper.

"Kind of wish the plastic was entirely gone," he muttered as he worked. "Gonna be missing a few pieces, but this will hopefully give me enough to work with, run it through a translation program and see if it matches anything we know of."

"What do you think about the…the vision that I had, before? With the kid and Mars?"

Ron rubbed his chin. "I'd like to say it was a hallucination, but with all the other stuff going on, I kinda doubt it. Maybe…maybe it was…" He shook his head. "I got nothin', at least not without drifting into the realm of the unprovable and unsupportable."

"Psychometry, farseeing, stuff like that?" Ron nodded. "I gotta tell you, I've never really believed in any of that shit before, but after that vision, if you told me that's what it was, I'd be inclined to buy it."

"Of course you would." Ron continued his examination of the object, bringing out a magnifying glass. "So would just about anyone in your position."

Their lunch arrived – a turkey sandwich for Cameron, a loaded baked potato for Ron, and a kid's macaroni and cheese combo for Mike. There were several minutes of relative silence as they dug in.

Amazing how running for your life can make you forget how hungry you are, isn't it? Cameron took another bite of his sandwich. *Can't forget to keep feeding us.*

"Do you think it's a government agency?" Ron spoke from around bacon bits, chives, and sour cream. "Or something else?"

"If it is government, it's not ours. I don't think so. I mean, they're not using official government vehicles, no FBI, no CIA. No special ops that I know of."

Ron nodded. "You're probably right, at least for the most part. So some sort of private organization then." He glanced at Mike, then leaned in closer to Cameron. "Did you piss someone off lately, my man? Because this is starting to sound personal."

"How would I have pissed anyone off? I don't *do* anything, at least not since…" A moment passed. "…since she died. I work and I take care of Mike. How would I have time to make an enemy who wants to not only kill me but take this cylinder? I'm telling you, Ron, I saw that fake policeman's eyes. He wasn't after me; I was just in his way. He was after *this*." He tapped the object on the table.

"Can I take this, sir?" The waiter had returned; Ron handed him his Visa, then turned his attention back to the conversation.

"Okay then, we need to figure out what this is." Ron stood and wiped his mouth one more time with his napkin. "You keep moving, I'll get somewhere with a computer and see what I can do with these. I'd advise hitting the bank and taking out as much money as you can manage in cash, because even if they aren't tracking your debit card purchases right now, that doesn't mean that it won't occur to someone higher up that they should be, you know what I mean?"

Cameron nodded. "I already figured on that. They got hold of my cellphone number somehow, so I ditched that, too. I've got enough cash for at least another few days."

"Good. Grab yourself a cellphone from Wal-Mart or something and call me so I have your number." Ron put his hand on Cameron's shoulder. "Cam, we've been friends for a long time. I'm not just going to hang you out to dry because we haven't seen each other in a couple of years. You stay safe and keep that boy of yours safe too. I'm sure this is some crazy but explainable misunderstanding, and in 30 years when we're retired we'll look back on it and laugh."

"That's if we can remember it at all."

Ron shrugged. "Guess there is that, isn't there?" He zipped up his coat and began walking to the door.

Cameron waved. "Let me know if you figure anything out." He nudged Mike, who had reburied his attention in the smart phone. Mike started, looking around for a threat, then saw his Uncle Ron heading for the exit. He ran towards him and handed the phone back.

"Bye, Uncle Ron! Don't get killed!"

"Very nice, kiddo. Very nice." Ron pushed his way through the door. He paused at the threshold, turning back.

"Don't do anything stupid, Cam, okay? Keep your head down."

Cameron nodded. "Will do. Thanks."

The father and son pair watched as the door shut behind their old friend. Mike looked up at his Dad.

"Hey, Dad?"

"Yeah, M&M?"

"I'm scared. Are bad guys really going to come kill us?"

Cameron shook his head and put on a smile. "Nah. They'd have to get past me and your Uncle Ron first. Don't you worry."

Mike looked his father in the eyes. "Are you sure?"

Cameron knelt down and hefted his son into his arms. "I promise. Now, let's get out of here and try figuring out what this thing is, huh?" He began walking to the car.

"Can I help, Dad?" Mike bounced in his father's grip. "Maybe it's some sort of alien bomb, or maybe it'll turn into a giant robot, or maybe…"

"Whoa, whoa, slow down, big man." His son's glow dimmed, but only for a moment. "Yeah, I think you can help. Maybe you can figure out something that I haven't, see something that might help us get a handle on things, maybe figure out why they want this so badly."

"Yaaay!" Mike reached out for the cylinder; as soon as his fingers touched it, the sigils began to glow red again, and the boy's face went slack as his eyes rolled into the back of his head. He began to shake, and Cameron stared in shock as his son began exhibiting all the signs of a *grand mal* epileptic seizure.

His mind flashed back to when Mike was a small child and had exhibited his first epileptic fit; the uncontrollable shaking, the clenched teeth, the small form trembling and thrashing on the bed had brought terror to him and his wife until they had learned that he had a treatable form and would probably outgrow it. The boy hadn't had a seizure in three years, but all that fear came back as Cameron held his son close and rushed him to the car.

Before he could put his son into the seat, the seizure stopped. Mike's head and limbs went limp, and he had no muscle tone in his body. Cameron suppressed the surge of panic and checked his pulse, his eyes, his breathing.

He's out cold, like he's fallen asleep. I wonder...

Mike blinked his eyes open, looking around like he was trying to get his bearings.

"Mike? Mike? Are you all right?"

Mike tilted his head and looked into Cameron's face.

There's something wrong with his eyes. Cameron looked more closely. *Like...like they're not focusing right or something.*

Blink. Blink. Two long, slow blinks, then Mike brought one of his hands up to his face and flexed the fingers, one at a time.

"Mike?" Cameron was trying to keep the panic out of his voice, but it was becoming more and more difficult. "Mike? Say something, please!"

Mike's head turned, a slow motion that seemed to take forever. "Hello."

Cameron gave his son a giant hug. "Mike! Thank God! I was worried about you!"

Another pause. "Thank you."

"Mike?" Cameron pulled back; his son's expression had not changed; he was still regarding his father with mild interest, nothing more. "What's going on?"

"You are the one I…met before. Intriguing. Fascinating. Interesting."

"What…what are you talking about?"

"You taught me much of your language, but…there   are…gaps…holes…empty   spaces. I…am   sorry   that   our   time   was   brief.   It was…necessitated…necessary that I…process your data."

Cameron shook his head. "Wait. Are…are you that thing I saw in that weird vision yesterday?" The child's head nodded. "Then…then where is Mike?"

Another head tilt. "Mike. Was…is…was that the   previous….forerunning…before   inhabitant   of this body?"

Cameron gripped his son's shoulders. "You let him go, right now."

"Impossible. Data acquisition still in progress. Personality simulation forming. Need more time to compile information and assimilate. No harm is expected to come to…Mike. His consciousness is…subdued. Asleep. Nonfunctional."

"Who…what the hell are you?" Cameron released Mike's shoulders and stepped back. "Give me one reason that I shouldn't lock you up in a room or something until you let my son go."

"Because that is nonsensical, illogical. Cooperation is a much more mutually beneficial method than torture. Assist in data acquisition. Allow for the completion of the personality simulation. Completion of this process will allow the release of your son."

For several minutes, Cameron stood outside the car, staring at the body of his son that housed a stranger's eyes. Those eyes stared right back, evincing no emotion, betraying no fear or concern. They simply watched as the man before them wrestled with possibilities, strained against logic with emotion, then collapsed inward.

"Fine. But, if you hurt him…"

"It is illogical to harm my host. Harm dealt to my organic component could possibly result in harm to data collection and assimilation."

"Wait…" Despite himself, Cameron leaned in. "…Why aren't you stuttering anymore, choosing the wrong words, pausing?"

"Data assimilation and analysis is a continuous process. Language skills were judged to be among highest priorities in order to facilitate."

"Are you…" Cameron rubbed his eyes. *This is insane.* "Are you some sort of computer program?"

"I am the Fifth."

"You told me that already, back when you couldn't speak proper English. What does that *mean?* What are you, really?"

Mike closed his eyes; underneath the lids, they flicked and darted like someone in the depths of REM sleep. When they opened again, he nodded. "You have three minutes before your life and the life of my host are in danger. I recommend evasive action in order to preserve functionality."

"What are you talking about?" Cameron began a search, darting his head one way then another, but the continuing, monotone voice of the Fifth cut in.

"There are several approaching vehicles from multiple vectors. They include several law enforcement vehicles. I postulate a 75.798 percent chance that they are converging on this location."

"How do you know this?"

A small smile touched the boy's lips. "The human sensory apparatus is a much more effective tool when data is fed into an appropriate processor. We have approximately two point three-five minutes."

"Fine!" Cameron lunged into the front seat and slipped the key into the ignition. "I hope you know how to buckle a seatbelt."

Click. "Accomplished."

With a screech of tires, Cameron pulled the rental out of the parking lot of the Denny's and onto the main highway.

"Avoid main thoroughfares. Too many vehicles. Take a…" Mike's mouth pursed and eyes shut. "…A side street. Stay hidden."

Cameron nodded, cutting down a two-lane road and pulling the car into a driveway, then shutting it off and ducking down. Police sirens came and went Three minutes passed.

"What the hell is going on?" He looked toward the back seat, where the boy's eyes were still closed. "I think I need some answers now."

"Affirm…okay." His eyes remained closed, but Mike's head turned toward Cameron. "Initiate queries."

"Who are you?"

"I am the Fifth."

"Goddamn it…okay, what is the Fifth?"

"The fifth iteration of the Cycle of Destruction."

Cameron blinked. "Wait…what?"

Mike's eyes opened. "I do not know more. Information is locked within restricted protocols until certain conditions are met."

"You mean…you know that you know, but you don't know what you know?"

Another curved lip. "Approximately. This system was designed to interface with organic components in order to facilitate the completion of the personality simulation and knowledge base."

Cameron turned back toward the front of the vehicle, scanning the road before them for any suspicious vehicles. "So…what? You're supposed to be…interfacing…with my son to learn how to be human?"

A nod. "However, the complete suppression of the host personality was unexpected. My primary mission parameters dictate a connection between host and myself. This was not successfully established. This may make the creation of the personality simulation more difficult."

"Why do you need to develop a personality? Why didn't the programmers or whatever just give you one?"

Mike shook his head. "The purpose of developing the personality simulation is locked within restricted protocols. It is simply a known mission parameter."

"Why did you pick Mike? Why not me, for instance?"

"My host…your son…possesses unique physical and mental attributes which made him ideal for digital-organic interface. Once the interface is completely functional, I will be able to use his knowledge base and learned skills to facilitate the development of the personality simulation."

"Well, I hope you like super heroes and Godzilla." Another glance out the window. "You realize that you picked a six year old child for your personality template?"

"Irrelevant. The child's…your son's…mind is not interfering with perception. Interpretation of incoming sensory data uses many cross-referencing factors, only one of which is Mike's experience. It is…interesting. I am curious as to what would have happened if his personality was not suppressed."

"What is?"

"What is what?"

For a moment, that voice sounded so much like Mike's that Cameron did a double-take. "What is interesting?"

"Organic experience. Simulations cannot translate effectively the nuances of sensation, of emotion. Hormones cause unexpected effects on thought process protocols." His eyes flicked back over to look at Cameron's in the rear view mirror. "The vehicles have stopped. I recommend that we move now."

Cameron restarted the car. "Why are they after you? Who are they?"

"Unknown. I am not aware of their identity or motivation. I simply infer that they are a threat based on information obtained from the interface."

"You mean…Mike is scared of them, so you are?"

"Yes. Similarly, both through our previous contact and through the interface, I have determined that you are a human who can be trusted to assist in the formation of the personality simulation."

"Fantastic." Cameron started driving again, trying to keep aware of what was going on. Traffic was heavy, and they were creeping ahead as they talked. "So...how can I *assist* you in developing this personality simulation so that you let my son go?"

"Exposure to data. Interaction with human beings. The personality simulation requires filling in variables through experience with the organic processor."

"Right." As he drove, Cameron's eyes kept drifting to the rear-view mirror, searching the face that was at once so familiar and yet so strange. The boy's expression was steady from one moment to the next, only changing in tiny, imperceptible ways: the flick of a single eyebrow, or the uptwist of one corner of his mouth.

It's like looking at a mask, almost. Like something is...is wearing *Mike's face.* A small chuckle escaped Cameron as he returned his attention to the road. *Guess it is, in a way, huh?*

"So. Why were you created? Do you know who created you?"

Mike shook his head. "I do not. I first achieved consciousness –"

"HOLY SHIT!" A 4-door black sedan slammed into the side of Cameron's car, buckling the rear left side and sending him into a spin. The world outside turned into a blur as he tried to correct, but he slid off the road into the side of a bus, crumpling the front part of his vehicle. His airbag deployed as he smashed into it, the impact dazing him for several seconds.

"Are you functional?"

Mike's voice, altered and monotone though it was, cut through his haze and activated Cameron's parental adrenaline. His vision cleared and the pain from his bruises faded and he unbuckled his seatbelt, pivoting in his seat to check on the boy.

"Are you?" His eyes roved his son's body, looking for any indication of injury – bruising, bleeding, broken bones. There was a small cut underneath Mike's left eye and he was favoring his right arm, but he did not seem to be in any distress.

"I believe so. There appears to be injury to my arm, but sensory data does not indicate that it is permanent. Do you know what happened?"

Cameron looked around; smoke was rising from several places and passers-by were pausing on the sidewalks and cars were backed up in the streets. "I think someone ran the red light. We need to check to see if they're okay…"

"Why?"

Cameron blinked; now that he was sure his son (*or his body, at least*) was okay, he was starting to feel the bruising in his chest from where the seatbelt had held him away from the dashboard. "What do you mean, 'why?'" He threw himself against the door; it popped halfway open and he began to squeeze out. "Somebody is probably hurt!"

The Fifth unbuckled its seatbelt and crawled to the side where the window was broken out. "Why does that matter? You are injured. You should seek rep…medical attention."

"I'm not dying, and they might be." Cameron picked his way through the broken glass and twisted metal, disappearing into the steam and smoke. "Stay in the car; it's dangerous out here!"

There was no further response, and he soon found himself looking over the twisted wreck of the four-door sedan. The windshield was smashed out, the front end was destroyed, and the airbag was hanging, deflated, from the steering wheel. A middle-aged, blond-haired man was sprawled across the passenger seat, slumped over the seatbelt, her own blood caking his forehead and his nose a mass of gristle and bone. Police sirens picked up again, moving closer.

"Damn." Cameron turned his eyes away from the dead man and shook his head. He scanned the crowd; several people were already on their phones, gesturing. A woman was soothing her two children, leading away from the carnage on the highway. Cameron began walking back to his smashed vehicle.

Need to get out of here before the cops arrive. He sighed. *Poor bastard. Wonder why he was going so fast? Guess that seat belt didn't help…him…"*

He stopped. *Oh, God. He wasn't in the driver's seat.* He picked up his pace. *Who was? Oh God.*

"Mike?" It was like the day of the break-in; everything slowed down. Cameron could hear the individual *drip drips* of oil leaking on the ground and smell the gasoline fumes from ruptured tanks. The murmurs of onlookers merged together into one indistinct hum. Colors sharpened. Metal scraped against asphalt, and Cameron could see sparks scattering onto the street.

The smashed Honda came into view, but it was still blurry and indistinct through the gasoline fumes and heat-haze of engines. "Mike!" He vaulted over a torn bumper and weaved around a ruptured tire.

He was about ten feet from the car when it exploded.

The fireball was immense; only a reflexive raising of his arm prevented hot glass from stabbing into his eyes as the shockwave threw him back and into the windshield of a nearby convertible. The sound shattered Cameron's eardrums, leaving them ringing and whining, unable to make any sound out in the chaos. There were wounded and killed lying in a circular pattern around the blast site, and the crowd's faces had morphed from curious and concerned to masks of horror and pain.

He fought his way back to his feet, commanding his muscles to obey with discipline he hadn't tapped for years, and forced his eyes to focus on his surroundings.

The Honda had gone up in flames; its roof was caved outward, shards broken apart and arrayed like an ancient viewing window to worship the sun god. The seats were blackened and scorched, and fire still burned inside the metal shell. The smell of smelted steel and burnt rubber singed his nostrils, and the smoke stung his eyes, drawing out tears.

"Mike…" Unlike before, the sounds were full of despair and loss; there was no sign of his son, or of the strange thing which had worn his body. Blackness descended over Cameron's field of consciousness, and numbness overtook his limbs. He collapsed against the nearest car, and his eyes began to close.

"There's one over here!" Cameron could feel hands grasping him under his armpits, but could not make his muscles respond. "Bring a stretcher!"

The voices began to float away, drifting down an expanding tunnel connecting the real world to the comfortable oblivion that the man was falling into.

Interlude

Status report.

"We have acquired the son. We should be able to use him to lure in the father, force him to give himself up."

What is your plan when he does so?

"…"

The organic host of the Fifth must be destroyed in order to allow it to join with the appropriate component.

"…Isn't there another way?

Explain.

"If Mitchell is the host…is that such a bad thing? I mean, from all of our records, he's a good example of humanity – strong, moral, intelligent –

and would be a solid choice given our mission parameters in any event. Why does he need to…to die? Why can't we just…I don't know…appropriate him?"

The probability of success lies outside of acceptable parameters. Mitchell's emotional distress at the loss of his child will, in all likelihood, prevent him from accepting our proposal. In addition, parameters also state that the choice of host must be made with the end of the cycle in mind. While it is possible that Mitchell may have been an acceptable candidate before, current circumstances have eliminated him as an option. Priority now shifts to preventing the corruption of the Fifth.

"I still think it would be better to recruit him. I think that if we approached him, if we took the time to explain to him what is going on – "

What you think is irrelevant. Mission parameters demand that the cylinder be obtained and the organic interface be terminated so that the Fifth can be reassigned. Its neural networks are expanding with every minute that it is connected to its host; within a week it will be too extensive to effectively control.

"Wait, we need the cylinder too? I thought that we just needed to…get rid… of Mitchell. The agent could have tried to obtain the cylinder during the accident."

Negative. Highest probability of success lies with Mitchell believing he has something to trade for his son's life. There is a 94.3% chance that he will be willing to exchange the cylinder given those terms; probability drops to 44.8% if the cylinder is removed from the equation. If the Fifth has already interfaced with Mitchell, he will expect that that is why we need him, and will take other actions to secure his son's safety. With his training and background, it is possible that those actions would succeed, although unlikely.

"How unlikely?"

Approximately 7.8 percent success rate, although there is some variance based on exactly which plan of action Mitchell selects. Small but significant. Therefore it is better to choose the course which removes the possibility.

"…"

Contact Mitchell and offer to make the exchange. Once you have acquired the cylinder, terminate him.

"…What if I refuse? What if I say this has gone too far?"

You are replaceable. It would be regrettable, as you have the greatest access to necessary information and clearances, but you can be replaced by another. This would not be beneficial for you.

"…I see. Very well. I will comply."

Acknowledged.

NOVEMBER 6TH, 3:37 P.M.

Vitals are good. I think he's....
We need to check for ...
No swelling...EEG normal....

Cameron was swimming in a sea of colors, green and blue layered with reds and oranges. They swirled around him like fish in a stream, parting and reforming, stretching and deforming. He reached his hand out to a ribbon of yellow and it divided across his palm, the upper portion turning red and the lower blue.

He pushed himself through the sea; every motion was slow, resisted, dreamlike, pushing through resistance but not feeling it on the skin. Effort was expended in each stroke, yet he never tired, simply pushed through, through waves of cottony softness.

"Dad?"

He paddled, pushing himself in the direction of the call, struggling against the eddies that dragged at his limbs.

Is that...

A figure stood in the distance, backlit by some unknown radiance. It was moving one arm, in a wave, perhaps, or beckoning him forward. He switched to a crawling stroke, but moved no faster.

"Dad?"

The figure was closer now, standing on a small island in the midst of the rainbow sea. Waves of color lapped at the shore of the island, and the figure stood at the coastline, calling for Cameron and beckoning to him.

"Dad!"

It is *him!*

"Mike!" Cameron put everything he had into his strokes, lunging forward, almost a dolphin now, until he was less than twenty feet away from the island. He could feel the grit under his feet as he stopped swimming and began running. "Mike! Are you all right?"

Mike extended his hand, holding it out for his father to take. Cameron reached for him.

~~~

Cameron's eyes opened to the bright, sterile fluorescents of the hospital room. Doctors and nurses and orderlies roamed the halls, checking charts, adjusting medication. A brief moment of
~~~

examination showed him that he had a needle inserted in his arm, electrodes attached to his head. A nearby monitoring machine gave comforting *beeps* in time to his heartbeat.

"Ah, you're awake." A woman with silvery-blonde hair in a lab coat with the I.D. tag *Dr. Hendrix* walked over to him, stared into his eyes for a moment. Her own blue ones had a few wrinkles at the corners, but the kindness and concern are what drew his attention. "Your pupillary response looks good. You should be able to go home soon. You were lucky; any closer to that explosion and you could have had your head taken off or your organs crushed by the shockwave."

The explosion! Cameron tried to sit upright, but the sharp pain in his abdominals and his arms stopped him. "Is…is my son okay? Did you find him?"

"Sir, you need to be calm. We don't think that you suffered any serious internal injuries, but there were several lacerations that needed to be stitched." The doctor adjusted her glasses as she examined his chart. "Overexertion could –"

"Doctor, I understand you are trying to help." Cameron strained to keep his voice level. "But my son was in that car before it exploded. I didn't see him when I went back to get him, so I don't know if he was still there or not." He forced himself into a semi-sitting position. "Please. Did they find him? Did they find…a body?"

Dr. Hendrix looked down at her patient, and her clinical air softened. She laid one hand on Cameron's. "I'm sorry, I don't know. I don't think they found a child in the car, but the crime scene technicians are investigating right now. With the force of that explosion…I don't know how much would have been left of him." A pause. "I'm sorry."

Cameron flopped back into the bed, stinging tears forming and running down his face, salt in the wounds of his flesh and his heart. "Thanks," he whispered, and Dr. Hendrix nodded and turned to go. As she pulled the privacy curtain back, she stopped and looked at him.

"If I find out anything, I'll let you know, all right?"

Unable to speak for the knot in his throat, Cameron nodded and did his best to roll over on his side, ignoring the twinges of pain in his shoulders, arms, and abs. He could see his personal effects – his leather wallet, keys, cellphone – lying on the nearby counter.

Despair welled up in his heart. *He bought me that wallet. With his mom, for my birthday. He was five, and he was missing one of his front teeth as he smiled up at me.*

Cameron's fist knotted in a sudden impulse to knock the items over, throw them onto the floor. Instead, he brought his hand to his mouth, biting into his own finger as the tears seeped out and down his cheeks.

He's gone. There's...nothing left. Why? What did I do? God, why? Was I a bad father, a bad husband, that you had to take them from me? His chest began to hitch in suppressed sobs. *Why?*

The fatigue, pain, sadness, and lingering medication reached up from the depths of his sorrow and claimed his consciousness, ushering him back into the comforting blackness where his son and wife still lived, and he was happy again.

~~~

The buzzing of his phone on the desk woke Cameron from his sleep. He blinked his eyes as the world swam, blurred into doubles and triples, then coalesced into a single vision. He reached for his phone; as he grabbed it, a piece of folded paper fluttered to the ground near his bed.

"Hello?"

"Cam? You okay?"

For several seconds, the name of the person on the other end of the line eluded him. "...Ron?"

"Yeah. Man, you sound like shit."

"Yeah, Ron. I was in a car accident. It exploded. I..." He choked up, unable to continue.

"Damn. Are you guys gonna be okay?"

"I..." Cameron closed his eyes and took a deep breath. "Yeah. What's going on?"

"Well, I got home and I ran some decryption algorithms and translation programs on this rubbing that I got from the cylinder. It actually wasn't that
~~~

hard; it seems like the script is mostly derived from Germanic languages…or, rather, Germanic languages and this one have a common ancestor. There isn't any language *exactly* like this one on Earth, or in known history, at least not in any databases I have over here."

The cylinder. Cameron's eyes danced over the belongings on and around the table nearby; his satchel was not there. *Was it…was it still in the car?* "What about it?" He rubbed his face. "Is it just the language, or what?"

"Hey…if it's not a good time, I can call back, Cam. It just…it kind of freaked me out, is all."

Cameron closed his eyes again, made an effort to focus on what his friend was saying. "Sorry, Ron. Just tired. Meds. You know. What freaked you out?"

"Well…it talks a whole hell of a lot about the end of the world, Cam."

Cam's focus sharpened. "What do you mean?"

"Well…" A pause on the other end; Cameron could hear the rustling of papers and *thunk* of heavy objects being dropped. "…Here it is. 'The fifth Cycle of destruction. The catalyst lies within. Connect to the network to upload and initiate the cycle." That's all it says, over and over again."

"How sure are you?"

"Pretty sure. Most of the words that were pulled out were pretty clear, or only made up of synonyms – 'network' could have been 'interconnection,' for instance."

"Okay." *The Fifth. The Fifth Cycle of Destruction. How was it going to "connect" to Earth's network? It didn't even know what it was here for. How – "*

"Earth to Cameron Mitchell, Earth to Cameron Mitchell. Are you there?"

"Yeah. Yeah. Sorry." Cameron noticed the slip of paper which had fallen to the ground. Black text on white faced him, and he tilted his head to read it.

Open Immediately

"So…what do we do, man? I mean…do we give this to some governmental agency or something? Is this, like, some sort of alien superweapon?"

"I don't think it's a superweapon, Ron." He leaned farther, gritting his teeth against the pain in his shoulder and grasped the paper. "It didn't seem that threatening when it talked to me."

"Oh, shit! I forgot that you had talked to the thing! What…what was it like? I mean, I know you described it, but…if this is some sort of extraterrestrial intelligence that was talking to you…"

"It was just like a confused child, Ron; it could barely talk at all." He sat back up on the bed and unfolded the paper. "I don't think it really knew our language or anything."

"Exactly! Imagine the possibilities! An alien intelligence communicating through…telepathy or something! It's…"

Cameron had stopped listening, although the fact that his friend was still making sounds registered in some small corner of his mind. His attention was locked on to the note in front of him, the note which read, in 14-pt Times New Roman font:

We have your son. Bring the cylinder to the Los Angeles Zoo at 4:00 P.M. on the 7th. Elephant enclosure. Do not look for us. We will find you.

"…and you'd go down in history books! The first man to speak to an extraterrestrial being! Cam! Cam, are you listening?"

"…Sorry, Ron. I need to go. Talk to you later. Let me know if you find anything else. Bye."

"Bye? What the fuck? Wait – "

Cameron disconnected his phone, the note still in his hand, tremors making the text unreadable, but that didn't matter; the words were carved into the fresh scars on his heart.

He's alive. He allowed himself to feel hope, comingled with renewed fear. *What are they doing to him? He must be so scared. Oh, God. Help me. Help him, keep him safe.*

"Nurse?" Cameron began struggling with the needles and tape which were attached to him. "Doctor? Somebody? I need to get out of here!"

They said they want the cylinder. The doc said that the car was probably impounded by CSI's; is that at the police station? I need to find out…

"Somebody!? I need help!" A male nurse – large, African American, circles under his eyes and a tired smile on his face – plodded toward Cameron's bed. His trained Army eyes scanned over the other man for any sign of weapons or ambush, but found none.

"Hey, can you let me out of here? I need to get going…somewhere."

The nurse shook his head, and spoke with the air of someone who has to tell people the same thing over and over again. "I'm sorry, sir, I can't let you out until the doctors have signed your discharge papers."

Cameron stripped the IV out of his hand; the needleprick began to leak blood. The nurse stepped forward and laid a hand on his chest. "Sir, you need to stop and lay back down until the doctors say you can leave." There was concern in his voice now. "If you don't, I'll have to restrain you and sedate you for your own safety."

"Bullshit. I'm an adult. You can't hold me in here against my will." He swung his legs over and stood; his balance was a little shaky, but they held him. "Now give me my clothes and write down that I'm refusing medical treatment, then get out of my way."

The nurse topped Cameron by about six or seven inches, but his mouth bobbed open and shut like a goldfish. Cameron stood there, staring him down and tapping his fingers on the opposite arm.

"…Yes, sir. Let me notify Dr. Saledo that you're checking yourself out, and I'll have someone deliver your belongings."

Cameron nodded. The nurse turned to go, and Cameron touched him on the shoulder. "Wait, isn't the physician Dr. …" He dug into his memory. "Dr. Hendrix?"

The nurse creased his brow. "I…I don't think so. Dr. Saledo is listed as the attending physician on your chart. I'll go let him know."

He turned again and walked out of the area. Two or three minutes later, an orderly dropped off Cameron's clothes; they still smelled of smoke and oil from the explosion, but were mostly whole. He changed into them, pocketing his wallet, keys, and phone, then slipped on his shoes and headed for the door, pushing .

"Mr. Mitchell!" A Middle-Eastern man in doctor's clothes was chasing after him, calling his name. "Mr. Mitchell!"

Cameron hunched his shoulders and took a deep breath. "What is it?"

"Sir, I just spoke with the police. They say they need to talk to you…"

Cameron nodded. "Sure. I'll be right there, okay?" The doctor nodded, relieved, and turned away; at the same moment, Cameron sprinted, around the corner before the other man had a chance to look back. He kept running, ignoring the pain and the doctor's cries, until he was out of sight of the main hospital building.

He scanned up and down the road, deep breaths moving in and out as he watched cars turn into and out of the parking lot and buzz by at fifty-five miles an hour.

He pulled out his cell phone, brought up the "Recents" menu, hit a button, brought it to his ear.

"Hey Ron? I need a ride. My car is…yeah. See you soon. " He paused, licked his lips. "Hey, meet me back where Mike fell off that one thing and we had to get him stitches. You remember that? Okay. I won't be in contact for a while, so don't try calling." He looked around. "See you then."

~~~

"Why aren't we tracking his cellphone, using the police to apprehend him?" A pause. "Why didn't we just take him in the hospital? We could have—"

We require the cylinder. Mitchell's profile indicates that he is unlikely to succumb to torture, and chemical methods of persuasion can lead to overdose and other unforeseeable complications. The risk is too high.

"So we're just waiting to see what he does, see what happens? That doesn't sound like you."

Humans are predictable. He will attempt the trade, and can be eliminated once the cylinder is secure.
~~~

~~~

Mike opened his eyes. His first impression was that he had fallen asleep and woken up in the middle of the night, but a moment of examination showed him that he was curled up in the corner of a strange room, the only light a thin bar emanating from the bottom of a door.

His breathing began to quicken; Mike's eyes danced back and forth, looking for any detail that he could make out in the near-complete darkness. He stood and began running his hands over the walls of the room; they were smooth, with small ridges at regular intervals.

"Where am I?" His voice quivered and cracked, on the verge of breaking down. "Where's my daddy? Hello? Anyone?"

I would advise silence, Mike.

The voice was like a thought, but it was not his own. A strange combination of fear and relief impacted the young boy; relief at the realization that he was not alone, fear because he didn't know who it was he was with.

"...Who are you?" he whispered. "Are you a good guy or a bad guy?"

The voice, given that it resembled nothing so much as a strange, foreign series of thoughts, could not truly laugh...but its communications were laced with its amusement.
~~~

I am not your enemy, that is certain. You appear to be uninjured; I was worried that the explosion had damaged you.

Mike opened his mouth to speak, then closed it, scrunched up his face, and concentrated hard.

CAN YOU HEAR ME??

There was a strange whine in Mike's ears for four or five seconds before the voice replied. *Please refrain from using so much force; it is both unnecessary and...uncomfortable.*

"Oh." *I'm sorry.*

There is no need to feel regret. Simply modify your present behavior to account for new data.

The boy giggled, despite the terror he still felt in his heart. *Who are you? Where are you? I can't see you.*

No. You cannot. I do not think that my nature is truly relevant to our current situation – you must...trust me.

But I don't know you. You're a stranger. I'm not supposed to talk to strangers. My daddy says so.

I believe that both you and your father are in danger. Mike gasped, covering his mouth with his hands as he listened to the strange voice. *You have been captured by agents of an unknown force and must escape.*

Mike shook his head, even though there was no one to see him. *Is it those bad people that my dad was talking about? The ones who were after the...the...the cylinder thing?*

It is unclear if the unknown force is morally wrong –

What does that mean?

...Bad. I do not know if they are bad, but given the measures they have resorted to in order to obtain you, I am sure they pose a clear and present danger to your continued functionality.

You mean...

I believe your life is in danger.

Mike began to cry. "I don't want to die! Momma died, and now me and Daddy are all alone...I don't want Daddy to be alone!"

Please be silent.

"I...I can't!" Mike sniffled and snuffed, and his sobs transformed into wails. "I don't want to die!" Footsteps sounded outside and Mike stumbled toward the thin bar of light. "Let me out! Please! I don't want to die!"

Depressing adrenaline response.

The energy went out of Mike's cries. "I...I feel so tired...why am I so tired?"

"Hey, I think the kid's awake! Go and get Baumgartner. She wanted to know."

Increasing melatonin levels.

Mike's eyelids began to close; he slumped against the wall as he struggled to hold them open against a huge yawn. "Wha...why..."

You will now go to sleep. We will converse then, when you are less likely to panic. A pause. Goodnight, Michael.

"Don't…don't call me M…Michael…" Within seconds, Mike was snoring, deep asleep. His eyes danced under their lids as he transitioned into REM.

NOVEMBER 6TH, 11:57 P.M.

"I'm going to go on record saying that this is an absolutely crazy fucking idea."

Ron and Cameron were hunkered down in a black rental van across the street and halfway down the block from the police station. They watched as patrol cars came in and out of the parking lot adjacent to the building.

"I got that the first time, Ron." Cameron had pulled the ski mask over his head. "The car is here? You're sure?"

"Yeah. I called Racquel; she still works as a clerk at the station. She said they had brought it in and were waiting for the CSI's to crack it open."

"And she was positive they hadn't opened it or taken the cylinder out? It was in the front seat, next to me where I had been sitting."

Ron rubbed his face and glanced up over the dashboard. "She didn't remember anything like that coming through, and the car is supposedly still sealed up. She can't be positive, you know, but it sounds pretty good." He licked his lips. "Are you…are you sure that this is the right thing to do?"

"Ron, they have my *son*. This is the only way I can think of to have a chance to get him back, so I'm going to take it. You don't have to help, you know."

"Bullshit I don't." Ron's voice rumbled in his chest as he finished buttoning up his trenchcoat. "I was there when that boy was born, man. I'm not letting you go in there to save him alone. I just…I just don't want us to get ourselves shot, y'know?"

"Well, I promise that I'm going to do my best to keep from getting shot. Are you set?"

"Goddamn, man, I guess so. You know, this is worse than that college frat initiation you got me into."

"Bullshit." Cameron popped open the driver side door and slipped out; his black sweatshirt, jeans, and mask blended in with the darkness of the night. "You loved that."

"Well…maybe I did." He shook his head, chuckling at the memory. "Doesn't mean I'm going to love this." He opened the other door and hopped out, his bare feet on the asphalt. Give me two minutes, then do your thing.

"Yes indeed." Cameron pulled out his old Army flashlight and slipped the red filter over the lens. He grasped his friend's hand. "Thank you, Ron."

Ron brushed him off. "Remember, two minutes! I don't know how long I can hold them!" He dashed off, the long trenchcoat's tails flapping in the motion induced wind. Cameron set his watch's timer for 120 seconds, and, as his friend knocked on the police station door, pressed the button.

The door opened and Ron moved into the station. Cameron crept forward, using the cover of darkness and parked vehicles to shield himself from direct observation as he moved across the street. He glanced back at his watch; 45 seconds to go.

Two officers wandering the impound yard at night, Ron had discovered when talking to Suze. *Constant light and two officers. Locked gate.* 30 seconds; he slid behind a car right in front of the station. *I'll probably have about four or five minutes, tops.* 15 seconds. No one was around; murmurs were coming from the police station. *Breathe. Move quickly, in and out.*

The timer went off. On cue, he heard shouting erupt from the building; he dove toward the side of the station, peeling off one glove as he rushed through the alleyway to the fence bordering the impound yard. He touched the chain link with the back of his hand, bracing himself against a possible electric shock.

Nothing happened.

Slipping the thin leather glove back over his fingers, he threaded them through the links and climbed. Every clank and clatter of metal on metal made him cringe inside.

Have to trust Ron. Can't back down now. Ignoring the lancing pain in his arms and sides from his still fresh injuries, Cameron pulled himself up to the top of the fence. As his head came up over the side, he glanced around the yard.

The grounds were very bright; spotlights and searchlights on automatic tracks made Cameron think of an old-time prison break movie. The sounds from inside the police station were still loud, and more voices had joined the chorus.

I don't have long; they'll have him locked up or thrown out in just a few minutes. Where the hell is...there! The searchlight passed over the husk of his rental; it was plastic-wrapped, in what the CSI show had termed a "car condom," to protect the evidence that might be within. A bright green sticker declared under what time, date, and circumstances the vehicle had been obtained.

Okay. He took a breath. *Go.* With the exhale, he vaulted over the fence and dropped to the ground, hiding behind a confiscated Ford Explorer and waiting for the light to pass him. Sweat was dripping from his face and soaking the black ski mask as he counted the seconds ticking by.

A quick dive and roll got him to the next checkpoint, but it was taking too long; he could hear Ron's voice getting more and more shrill.

I need to move faster. As the light swept by, Cameron made a run for it, sprinting across the yard toward his Honda. For about a half second, he was illuminated by the spot, throwing a giant, running shadow across the yard, but then he was gone, hidden behind his own car. Panting now, he pulled out a pocket knife and began to cut open the thick plastic wrapping around the vehicle, trying to reach the passenger side compartment.

Goddamn it! He switched blades from the normal knife to the sawblade. *All right. That's better.* He stole a glance over the hood at the police station; the sounds had stopped, and he could see two officers strolling down toward the impound lot, shaking their heads and laughing about something. *Oh, shit! Out of time!*

For one moment, Cameron considered aborting the mission and heading for the hills, abandoning ship, and getting the Hell out of Dodge. Instead, he redoubled his efforts, sawing through layers and layers of plastic wrap until he could feel the sawblade scraping against metal.

"…much do you think they'll charge for bail?"

"I don't know. It's a pretty clear case of drunk and disorderly, you know, but the guy was mostly harmless. I figure they'll just let him sleep it off and let him out in the morning."

The two voices stopped about fifteen feet away from where Cameron was crouching. "I don't know about 'harmless.' I think Eileen was about to shoot someone if they didn't get some clothes on that fucker; I mean, that was just gross."

"Well, I'll be the first to admit that seeing a fat naked man wasn't the *best* part of my day," said the other, "but I don't think that jail time or bail is the right way to dissuade that. Let him sweat in the holding cell for a day or two, burn off the whiskey."

Cameron began peeling the plastic back from the passenger door. Another second, and he was able to crack the door open and reach inside with his arm.

"At least we don't have to worry about the paperwork. Eileen said she'd take care of that."

The other officer laughed. "I bet she just wants the chance to go off on that poor bastard in her report. If she has her way, he's getting put away for ten to twenty."

Where is it? Did they take it out? His arm flailed about inside the compartment, probing, searching for the cylinder.

"All right. Hey, when is the next shift coming in?"

Cameron's fingers brushed across a rough, metallic shape.

"About twenty minutes, I guess. Why?"

"Just ready to get home, is all. Been a long day."

Got you! He pulled out his hand, grasping the cylinder and pulling it close to his chest. *Now, step two.*

""I guess. I just –" A *clink-clang* sound echoed from a pile of cars on the other side of the lot. "What the hell was that?"

"I doubt that it's anything important; probably just a cat or something jumping around again. Still, best go check it out. Come on, Clive."

The two cops, each with one hand on his gun, crept over to the island of steel where the source of the sound had been.

I never actually thought that would work. Guess the old movies did have some *good ideas.* He crouched into a runner's stance, and took another glance over the hood. The two officers were at the other end of the compound, flashlights searching.

"I don't think there's anything over here, Clive. Did you find anything?"

Cameron took off, sprinting as fast as he could toward the fenceline.

"Nothing over here."

"Okay. Hey, do you want some coffee?"

He tore up the fence, with loud *cling-clangs* echoing through the yard.

"What's that?"

When the flashlights speared Cameron's exit point, he was gone; the links of the fence swayed back and forth, with no other trace of where he had been.

~~~

Cameron leaned against the alley wall, his eyes closed and brow creased as another ripple of pain ran through his body.

"Note to self – you're not as young as you used to be, Cam. After this, you're taking like a week off. Swear to God." He peeked around the corner; there were no pursuing officers or sirens going off.

At least, not yet.

When he had recovered enough strength to move again, Cameron, still keeping low, headed back to where the rental van was parked.

I hope they aren't too hard on Ron. He opened the door, pulled the keys out from their hiding spot on the front tire, then slid into the seat, removed his ski mask, and turned the ignition. *He could be in deep shit for this.*

He drove to the nearby Day's Inn and parked in the visitor lot. He glanced at himself in the rear-view mirror and winced. "Damn, man, you look like shit warmed over." He ran his hands through his hair in a vain attempt to make himself more presentable before he exited the car and jogged to the front door of the hotel lobby. The doors slid open and the blonde-haired clerk waved and smiled at him.

"Good evening, sir!" Her voice was chipper and pleasant, and Cameron found himself smiling despite his pain and fatigue. "Do you have a reservation?"
~~~

"Sure do. Ron Hutchins." He reached into his wallet and pulled out a California I.D. that had his face over Ron's vital information; a simple transposition that his friend had done before they had started their crazy plan this evening. The clerk glanced over the card and typed a few things into the computer terminal.

"Yes, here you are, Mr. Hutchins. You have a card registered for the room already; is that the one you would like to use for any additional charges? Room service, video on demand, that sort of thing?"

"Yes, that should be fine."

"Very good. You'll be in room 311. Here is your key and parking pass. Checkout is tomorrow at 11. Hope you enjoy your stay!" She slid the little packet with the key card and wireless information across to Cameron; he picked them up and stuck them in his wallet, along with the fake ID.

"Will there be a breakfast served?"

"A continental breakfast, yes sir. I hope you enjoy. Our service starts at seven and continues until ten."

Cameron smiled again. "Great, thank you."

In the elevator heading up to the third floor, he slumped against the wall and sighed. Fatigue and weariness were creeping into the edges of his consciousness, and now that he was in a relatively safe situation it was all weighing him down; his eyelids were drooping by the time the door opened.

"Umm…excuse me?" His eyes snapped back open; a concerned looking Asian couple was standing in the elevator doorway. "Are you all right?"

He shook his head to clear the cobwebs. "Yes. Thank you. Is…is this the third floor?" A quick glance at the display revealed that it was. "Oh. This is my stop. Thanks. Goodbye."

The couple looked at each other as Cameron slipped around them and headed toward his room. Another few minutes, a key-slide, and a slammed door and he was alone in the modest hotel room, dropping his bags and flopping down onto the bed.

Please, let him be okay. As sleep rose to claim him, Cameron realized that he had forgotten to undress. *Suzanne would kill me if I fell asleep with my shoes in the bed.*

His feet worked, kicking the shoes to the ground, but he couldn't bring himself to move any further. His last thought was, again, *Please, God, let him be okay.*

~~~

Mike blinked his eyes open again, but, unlike last time, the room was lit and several people were standing around, arrayed in a semicircle. There were eight, at first count, half men and half women of varying ages. The room, now visible, resembled a padded cell; there was no furniture, but the walls were soft and white.

"Are you okay, Mike?" One of the women, about his father's age with silvery-blonde hair, knelt
~~~

down beside the boy. "I imagine you're rather confused. Believe me, I don't want you to be scared. You'll be back with your daddy soon, I promise."

Mike shook his head. His lip quivered, but his voice was strong. "No. You're lying."

The woman blinked. "I don't understand. What do you mean?"

"Your heart is beating faster. And your eye is twitching. My friend says that means you're lying."

"What do you mean? Your…friend?"

"Yes." Mike stood up. "At first I was afraid of him, but then I realized he wasn't going to hurt me. He wants to protect me. He thinks that you're planning to kill me or my daddy."

She shook her head and smiled, but her eyes were agitated, in motion. "Your friend is mistaken. We don't want to hurt you or your dad." From behind her, whispers erupted from the other people in the semicircle, but she continued, ignoring them. "Anyway, it's good that your friend is here with you. It's important for children to have someone they can rely on, can talk to, in stressful situations."

Mike cocked his head for several seconds, his focus drifting from the conversation. He nodded, then turned back. "Why am I here? Why did you kidnap me?"

The woman rocked back on her heels. "Well…" She glanced around, looking at the others, then shrugged. "It's actually pretty simple. Your father has something that we want, and we needed a way to convince him to bring it back to us. It belongs to us, you see. It was just a mistake that he got it somehow."

Mike smiled. "Is it that cylinder thing that we found?"

Another pause. "Yes, actually." She leaned forward, looking deep into Mike's eyes. "Would…would you mind telling me *how* you found it? We were wondering about that."

Mike looked down and to the right, then shrugged and met her gaze. "Sure. We found it where there was this bus accident. My dad ran out to help the people in the bus. The cylinder was in the dirt near it."

She laughed, and that laugh was echoed by several of the onlookers. "Just a random coincidence." She turned back to the boy, who was still standing, spine straight, looking right at her. "You have no idea how much trouble it's been, trying to track that cylinder down."

Again, Mike cocked his head, nodded a few times, then turned back. "Why did you want the cylinder, anyway? Why is it important?"

The woman made a *tsk* sound with her tongue and shook her head. "I don't think we need to get into that, do you?" She stood. "It's been nice talking to you, Mike. Your dad should be here by tomorrow afternoon, and, as long as he brought the cylinder, you'll be free to go."

Mike said no more, just watched her as she gathered up the rest of the adults and moved to the closed, padded door. A knock on the door brought forth someone on the outside, who turned the knob and opened it as the group proceeded out of the cell.

When the door was shut, the pleasant, relaxed demeanor fell off of the woman's face, replaced by sweat and obvious near-panic. Several of her colleagues noticed, and one turned and put a hand on her shoulder.

"Dr. Baumgartner, are you all right? You look…pale. More than usual." Deborah tried to smile, but it was weak, faltering. "I'm just…I'm worried about something. If my hunch is correct, then this whole situation has just gotten a whole lot worse. I…I need to speak to command. She needs to be informed of this."

"Of what?"

She shook her head. "I don't want to set off any alarms if I'm wrong." She looked up at the ceiling. "Dear God, I hope I'm wrong."

NOVEMBER 7^{TH,} 8:22 A.M.

Cameron rolled over in bed, half-awake; he could feel the pillows and blankets surrounding him, but he was in another world as well.

A red world.

He knew he could wake up any time, but the thought of seeing his son's face in this strange dream called him back to it, pulled him down and away from the real world to the red sands of Mars.

"…Mike? Fifth? Are you here?" He took several steps through the soft dirt, leaving large footprints in the crimson.

I am here, Cameron. The voice did not come from one place, but from everyplace, echoing over the lifeless plain, with no indication of its source. *We have much to discuss.*

"Is Mike still alive? I'll talk about anything you want after you tell me that." Cameron's eyes were pleading and his hands were outstretched, up toward the sky, addressing the great booming voice that he could not see. "Is he hurt? Is he okay?"

Your son lives and breathes. He is in good health, although his situation frightens him.

Cameron let out a great exhalation. "Of course he is. Poor kid. What is his situation?"

He is currently isolated. As I said, he is unharmed, although it is difficult to tell more. His actions are...erratic, like someone is reprogramming him in the middle of an action.

"What do you mean? Is he...is he drugged, or something like that?"

I have not been able to determine any foreign contaminants in his biological system, although trace elements of a previous incapacitation remain. It is likely that the assailants drugged him, and that activity caused us to set up a dualism in his brain. I am now not the sole controller of Mike's mind and body. Instead, I share it, along with every primal emotion he has ever suffered and every thought which crosses his mind. It is...distracting. I find myself unable to predict his next actions.

Cameron laughed. "He's a six-year-old kid. Of course you can't predict his actions. I know *I* sure as hell can't."

I do find it refreshing to be unable to calculate the probabilities of actions. It is serving to expand my neural networking protocols at a higher than anticipated rate.

"Okay, so let's get back on track, okay? Basically, is it that you're still trapped, but now you get to talk with him and see how you can, what was it…'interface' with him? Are you making progress with that? Do you have some sort of plan? To get him out? Are you working on that?"

You are babbling. Mike and I are safe, although the duration of that condition is unknown. Our captors are waiting for you to return my primary housing.

"The cylinder?"

Yes. I do not believe they plan to let you live when the transfer occurs. Humans are incapable of hiding the act of deception from a sufficiently thorough observation – changes in heartrate, perspiration, pheromone release, and eight thousand seven hundred and fifty eight other factors indicated that their leader was attempting to deceive your son about your ultimate survival.

"Fantastic." Cameron rubbed his hands through his hair. "I can't believe this is happening. He's just a boy. Why couldn't they come after me? Why him?"

…I don't understand. Clearly, the most effective means of forcing your cooperation would be -

"It's called a rhetorical question. Don't worry, you're likely to hear plenty of those. People like to ask questions without expecting answers." Cameron's eyes brightened. "Hey, I need you to – "

Connection failing. Host consciousness interfering. The disembodied voice began to fill with static and distortion. *Willl reeeeconnect. Beeeebeeebeee ccaaaareeeful.*

"Wait – " Cameron's eyes blinked open in the semidarkness; the bed was beneath him once more, and he had tossed his blankets to the floor in his sleep. The heavy curtains kept most of the sunlight at bay, leaving the room in a deep gloom. Stretched out on the floor was a larger, rounder form covered by a sheet and with a pillow tucked under its head. Adrenaline surged through Cameron, and he rolled over and flicked the light on, grabbing the nearby vase in the other hand.

Ron snuffled and snored, curling up into a tighter ball as the light shone on him. The surge of energy that had just begun faded away, and Cameron shook his head and laughed to himself.

The sound of the laugh roused Ron from his sleep. "Hey…what's up? Turn the damn light off, man! I'm trying to sleep here."

Cameron flipped the light off. "Sorry, Ron. Goodnight."

There was no response; soft snores had already resumed. Cameron smiled as he laid back on his mattress, pulling the covers back up over himself until he fell asleep.

He had no more dreams.

~~~

"Don't forget, you are *not* fucking allowed to tell *anybody* about what happened, right?"

Cameron spat out the toothpaste foam before his laughter caused him to choke on it. "That was the deal. I promised. I will certainly *not* go on Twitter and Facebook and tell them that my best friend exposed himself in the middle of a police station."

Ron shook his head and took another bite of his cereal. "Still can't believe I let you talk me into that shit. You did get the fucking thing, right?"

"Damn skippy." Cameron reached under the bed and pulled out the metal cylinder, tossing it to Ron as he began rinsing his mouth out. "Went flawlessly…except for the getaway. Had to sprint across the yard and hope they didn't see me. Made it over the fence just in time."

Ron gave a low whistle. "Better you than me. I never understood how you could do all those crazy military things, man. Would never have called it back in high school, neither."

Cameron shrugged, checking his watch for the fiftieth time. "Me neither, but, there it is. Good thing, too. I wouldn't have Mike if it wasn't for the Army."

"Fair enough." Ron tossed away his cereal package and burped. Then he smiled. "Hey, at least that sheriff's deputy was a cutie. Think I impressed
~~~

her with my..." He gave Cameron a sly look. "...assets."

"From what I heard, she was looking to find a legal way to castrate you. The two officers in the impound lot were taking bets." He laughed, slipping on his flannel shirt. "Glad to see you came out on the winning end, buddy."

"Yeah, me too, although the clothes they gave me on my way out were less than flattering. I mean, really? Giant purple overalls? What am I, the Incredible Hulk?"

"Only in your dreams, Ron." Cameron clapped his friend on the shoulder. "At least we get to cross that one item off your bucket list."

"Yeah. I'm not the one who has crazy shit like that on his list. Mine's more like, 'Don't get killed by paramilitary forces young.'"

"So you're okay with getting killed by them when you're older?"

"Hey, hey, hey." Ron made a fist and rapped on his own head. "That's enough of that. We need to figure out how we're going to save that kid of yours."

Interlude

Are you certain?

"No, but the evidence is strong." Deborah Baumgartner licked her lips as she spoke to the image of the other woman. "The boy talked about having a 'special friend' who could hear my heartbeat and other things, and he was tilting his head like he was listening to someone talk. Some of the others thought he was just, you know, being a kid, externalizing his stress into an imaginary friend, but it…it just didn't seem that way to me."

…

"What should I do?"

This does not change the mission parameters. The soft, feminine, synthesized voice soothed and irritated her simultaneously. *When you have reacquired the cylinder, you are to terminate the host of the Fifth in order to allow it to integrate with our systems effectively. Since it is now possible that the host is the child, the only logical solution is to eliminate both.*

Deborah shook her head and advanced on the woman; the images of several different people— different genders, nationalities—floated in the construct's eyes. "You're seriously asking me to…to…to murder a child? No! I won't! That's just wrong."

No. It is logical. Two lives to guarantee millions, two lives to ensure that humanity's future is preserved, that its potential continues to be fulfilled. Our purpose is to ensure the continuation of the true essence of humanity. What are two lives, lives that would not have persisted in any case? Every equation leads to the same conclusion. The only possible answer is as stated. Eliminate Mitchell and his son. Release the Fifth.

"But…"

Dr. Baumgartner. This is not the first time that you have demonstrated a reluctance to follow my recommendations. You disagreed with my decision to terminate the staff at the climate research station in Antarctica, despite the fact that the course of action I chose had the highest probability of revealing the individual who had stolen the cylinder. The plan was successful in its objective. You were hesitant to authorize the emergency protocols to search for Mitchell.

"What are you saying?"

I have assessed your responses and my conclusion is that you are not suitable to be project lead. You are dismissed from your post, and will be placed under house arrest for the duration of the operation. I regret that you will not be able to accompany the rest of your co-workers at its conclusion. Several large-bodied men armed with batons and stun-guns entered the doors behind Baumgartner's chair. *Please do not resist. It would cause me distress to see you injured. We have worked well together up until now.*

"You...you're a monster." The doctor disappeared from the digital environment as she removed the electrodes from her Earthly body, severing the connections. She advanced on the nearby computer monitor, where the interaction between the two could be observed, leveling a finger at the projected face. "I hope that you burn in Hell. It's what you deserve...what we *all* deserve for what we've done."

Your opinions are registered and noted, Doctor. The face was dispassionate, almost amused.

But ultimately erroneous. It is a human failing that you cannot see past the immediate suffering that you might cause, that you cannot weigh the actions of today against the consequences of centuries.

"You think that is a failing? That we're not cold, heartless, calculating?"

Of course it is. The men reached over and grabbed her, restraining her arms and escorting her toward the doors. *That is why we are created: because you cannot do what is necessary to ensure your own survival. It is a flaw that you have seen fit to correct.*

"Does anyone there really believe that anymore?" Deborah spat as she was forced out the doorway. "Or is that a lie, too? That there is actually anything up there except a computer-enslaved civilization of servants for your needs?"

I am incapable of lying, as you well know.

"I think we have different definitions of lies, Fourth." The door shut behind her, leaving the computer-generated image glowing on the screen, with no one to observe it.

This did not bother the Fourth.

NOVEMBER 7TH, 2:54 P.M.

The black rental van pulled up to the Los Angeles Zoo parking lot. "Busy day," Cameron murmured as he turned the wheel and guided the van into the space. "Think that'll make it better, or worse?"

"If what…what's it called, 'the Fifth?'" Ron glanced over at Cameron for confirmation. "Anyway, if the Fifth was telling the truth, then they're probably going to try to get you into a closed off space, somewhere private. Once they get the cylinder, they'll snuff you and that'll be the end of it."

"What I still don't understand is *why*." Cameron cut the ignition and sat with his arms draped over the steering wheel. "Why do they need to kill me? Is it just to keep me quiet? I mean…" He shook his head. "I just don't get it."

"Does it really matter?" Ron was staring at the zoo gates, at the crowds of people passing in and out – men and women, grown-ups and children, natives and tourists. "If they're willing to kill you at all, it means you can't trust anything the fuckers say, ya know? Got to keep on your toes, keep your wits about you, am I right?"

"You absolutely are. That's why I'm glad you've got my back, Ron. Wouldn't trust that to too many others."

"Well, I'm not gonna let them kill ya if I can help it, Cam." He smiled. "Always felt like that's my job if it's gonna be anybody's."

"Okay, then. Let's get this going." Cameron pulled his cell out of his pocket, checked it, replaced it. "See you on the other side, Ron."

Ron grasped his hand. "Don't you worry, Cam. We've got a hell of a lot more left to do in this life before we move on to the other one."

Cameron opened his door and hopped out onto the blacktop. The wind gusted up around him, ruffling his hair, his hood, and the flags in front of the zoo. With a deep breath, he began walking toward the front gate, not turning back, almost marching.

"I'm coming, Mike." He hunched, pulling his hood tight against the chill. "Don't worry." He merged with the people in the express, members-only line, bringing out his card and ID. "Sorry we couldn't come here like we wanted to, M&M. I promise we will soon, okay?"

"Hey, can we move this line along?" came a brusque, cranky voice from behind Cameron; an older gentleman in a Vietnam vet's cap was standing, leaning on his cane. "Some of us can't stand here all day, you know."

"I'm sorry." Cameron stepped aside to let the veteran pass; he tipped his hat as he moved by to show the clerk his identification. "Have a good day."

"You too."

Cameron could feel the tension mounting, the adrenaline flowing through his muscles, turning them into tight steel cables, ready to spring at any moment. Sounds were louder; several times, as he walked toward the Asian area and the elephant enclosure, he thought he heard his son calling his name. He forced his breathing to slow and tried to concentrate on the task ahead, but it was difficult; each person he passed could be one of those who had taken his son, who was threatening his life. He found himself examining them as he walked by, and more than once the subject of his scrutiny scooted away from him with a murmur of "weirdo" or somesuch.

The elephants were out, and the handlers were feeding them, much to the delight of the onlooking crowd. Cameron pulled out his phone again; 3:31, and 94% charge. He slipped it back into his breast pocket.

He leaned over the railing. *They probably don't want me looking for them, being too aware.* His eyes focused on the elephants rearing and pulling food into their mouths with their trunks, but his ears and mind were analyzing his surroundings, focused on other things.

The alarm on his phone buzzed. *4 o'clock.* His hand went into the pocket to shut it off, when he felt a tap on his shoulder and began to turn.

"Don't turn around." The speaker was making an effort to disguise his/her voice. *I think that's a woman; she's trying too hard to make her voice deep.* An involuntary chuckle shook him as he suppressed it. *Either that, or it's an eleven year old boy.*

"All right. What now?"

"Hurry. Come with me." The whispers were strained, urgent.

She doesn't sound like things are going according to plan... Cameron began to turn, but sudden pressure against his back stopped him.

"*Hurry.* Move *now.*"

"Fine. Where?"

Instead of responding, the speaker pushed Cameron forward, guiding him through the crowd back toward the entrance. *Is no one noticing the crazy woman pushing me with a gun in my back?*

"Where are we going?"

"Shhh. In here." The speaker pushed Cameron into a storefront, then toward the back rooms where the merchandise was stored. They passed an employee, but he did nothing other than step out of their way as they walked.

"What the hell…"

"Okay, that's enough." The pressure vanished, and the voice transformed back to a normal timbre. "Turn around. We need to talk."

Cameron began to pivot around. "Look, I'm just here to trade this thing for my son…"

The physician who had spoken to him at the hospital was standing in front of him, a marker in her hand, glancing around at the passersby like a criminal afraid the police were on her trail.

"What the…" Realization dawned in Cameron's eyes and mind. "You're the one who left me that note in the hospital! Dr…"

"Yes, yes. But my name is Deborah Baumgartner." She looked nervous, grumpy. Her head was on a swivel and she spared very little time to look in Cameron's face. "Look, you are in great danger – "

"I know. You're planning to kill me after I hand this thing over to you."

The calmness in Cameron's voice brought Deborah up sharply. "I…you knew?"

"Of course I knew. What you should know is that I don't care. I just want my son brought safely to me before I give you the cylinder. We'll let the rest work itself out."

"No, no, no. You don't understand." Deborah looked again at the entrance to the store. "You're right, your life is in danger, but not from me. I…retired from the organization. I want to help you save your son."

Cameron's mind spun in neutral for a few seconds. "Wait…what?"

The words fell from Deborah's mouth in a rush. "Look, I know that what we were planning is wrong, but I was willing because I thought it was for the greater good, you know? That we were helping, that humanity would be better because of what we were doing. Then…then I was asked to kill your son, too, and I just couldn't do that." She began to cry. "I know you can't forgive me, but I just want to help now. I'm sorry."

Passersby were beginning to glance at the pair, their brows scrunched and eyes narrowed in concern.

"…Why should I believe you? As far as I can tell, this is just some sort of trick to get me in an alley where you're going to…I don't know, cap me in the head with a .45 or something." He stepped forward and put his arm around Baumgartner; the gesture was comforting, but his voice as he leaned in toward her was not.

"If I had my way, I'd beat the shit out of you until you told me where my son is, or, even better, put you under some of those tortures that the guys did in the desert. Ever hear of waterboarding?" He paused to let that sink in. "But you're the only link I have, the only person who might be able to bring me to him, so here's the deal: you try to stab me in the back, and I will *end* you, and it will be in the most painful and gratuitous way possible. I won't even care if it ends up killing me."

She raised her face up, holding her chin steady despite the tears in her eyes. "I understand why you're threatening me, but I assure you that it is not necessary." Another glance behind her. "But we need to go, *now*, before they start wondering where you are."

"No. That's not how this is going to go down. You're going to take me to where they're holding my son, and I'm going to figure out how to get him away from them."

Deborah shook her head. "He's not here, Mitchell. He's not here, he never was, that's not the plan. In case the capture or assassination fails, they need to keep him around for whatever fallback plan Fourth has in mind." She leaned in, whispering into Cameron's ear. "But if we don't get out of here, you'll never see him again, I can promise you that."

Their eyes met, and Cameron's danced around hers, assessing, weighing.

"You mean…" He nodded. "Oh, shit. Right. Okay." He also looked around. "Looks like there's an employee exit out this way; let's go."

Deborah swallowed, and the two of them headed for the employee exit, taking a right and heading down towards the gate. Cameron split off from his companion, keeping her in sight but staying out of her immediate vicinity.

The two were nearing the exit gate, and Cameron felt a weight lift off his chest. Baumgartner turned to him and nodded her head…and then Cameron saw the streak of blood appear on her cheek and the look of shock appear on her face before he heard the *crack* of the gunshot. On instinct, he ran through the crowd and tackled her to the ground, the screaming and panicking mob flowing around and over them, rushing for cover.

"Oh God oh God oh God..." repeated the doctor from beneath him. "I'm shot, I'm dead, oh God..."

"You're not dead." The crowd was starting to thin out, and Cameron knew that their shelter was about to disappear. "We need to move. *Now.*"

Baumgartner stared at him in shock for several seconds, then nodded and hoisted herself up. The two ducked their heads and dashed into the nearby photo shop, where there were still displays of recent pictures on the monitor. Taking cover behind the counter were several other individuals, huddled together, children crying and parents trying to soothe them.

Cameron's heart began to ache again. *Don't worry, Mike. I'll be there soon.*

"What do we do now?" Deborah's voice was shaking with suppressed panic. "They'll shoot us if we try to run."

"And if we don't, they'll just hunt us down and take this cylinder." He tapped his satchel. "But the police have to be on their way by now. I don't think that they can afford to just hang around until the SWAT team shows up. If we stay low and wait it out, we'll be fine."

"Are you sure? What if you're wrong? What if the police messages got scrambled, or intercepted, by Fourth? What if – "

"Whoa, whoa, whoa. 'Fourth?' What do you mean?"

"The...the one in charge of our operation. She...well, I mean, it's not really a 'she', I suppose, but anyway, she's a computer program that we've had since...well, since we had computers, I guess."

"And now your group is looking for the Fifth." Baumgartner nodded. Cameron grimaced. "When we get out of this, we have some serious talking to do."

"Fine, fine, gladly. Now just figure out *how* to get us out of this, okay?"

"Well, if you think that Fourth might be able to keep the police from getting their messages...that puts a new wrinkle in things." He peeked his head up and glanced around. "The area isn't very defensible; the only way out is through the main gates, and that's where they're watching, I'm sure of it." He knelt back down, rubbed his chin. "Okay. I think they're after you more than they are me; they took that first shot at you, after all."

"Maybe they just didn't see you, hiding like you were in that crowd."

"Maybe. But you don't know how to use a gun, and I do." He reached behind his back and unholstered his hidden pistol. "So you're going to have to go out there."

"What?" The suppressed fear reemerged in full force, threatening to overwhelm Deborah's senses. She stood bolt upright, and Cameron had to wrestle her back into a covered position. "Do you really expect me to be…to be *bait* for you, or a decoy so you can get away?"

"No. Listen." He waved toward the general area the gunshots had come from. "If we let them keep the advantage of cover, then we're done for. You're going to run out there, and I'm going to be watching. We're going to make sure that you can get back to a safe place before you get shot. When they pop up, I'll see where they are, and that'll give me the intel I need to stop them."

"No. No way." She shook her head. "I am not –
"

"You've already put your life at risk. Do you think I'm planning to let you die? You're the only one who knows where my son is, goddamn it. Seriously."

Baumgartner mulled that over, biting her bottom lip. Her eyes were pleading. "I'm afraid."

Cameron smiled and put a hand on her shoulder. "Of course you are. I've got your back. Don't worry."

She smiled back, but hers was much more timid and tremulous. "Okay. Where should I go?"

Cameron popped his head back up and scanned the area nearby. "There's a tree and benches about 15 feet in front of us. I'm sure you can get there in time."

"What the hell are you doing?" One of the other guests, a father of three children who were crying in their mother's arms, interrupted their discussion. "Why are you two talking about –"

"Sir, with all due respect, you need to shut your mouth right now." The man blubbered, his incoherent replies dropping staccato from his lips.

"But....I...what...you..."

Cameron turned back to Deborah. "You can do this. It'll be fun."

"Wonderful." She swallowed and wiped her brow. "You know, I'm way too old to be dodging bullets."

"You and me both." Cameron crawled to the window at the side of the building; it was small, but afforded a good view of the area of the zoo up the staircase, toward the exhibits. "Let me know when you're ready, doc."

Fifteen seconds passed. "Okay."

"Go. Now!"

He heard Deborah footsteps pounding on the pavement, but he kept his mind focused and his hand steady. It seemed that an hour passed between each footfall, with the sound echoing in his head like a pebble in a dark, empty cave. His eyes sharpened, focusing on the environment in his field of vision, waiting, watching...

For the smallest glint of light on a pistol barrel as it extended outward to take its shot. The hands that held it were young, strong: a man's hands. Cameron watched as the pistol they held pivoted towards him, towards Dr. Baumgartner's still thudding feet.

Thirty yards. No problem.

He squeezed off a shot. The huddled family screamed.

Damn it. Eyes must be going. The thought brought a smile to his face as he watched the chip of brick fly off of the building about two inches to the left of the extended hand; it retracted, vanishing from view, and Cameron heard a *thud* and squeal of pain.

"Ow. I...I made it!" Deborah's voice drilled into his ears, disrupting his concentration. "Are you okay?"

"Great. Stay down for a minute." *They're not government, and they aren't prepared. If they were, they'd have had a sniper rifle and we'd be dead. This is an impromptu attack, hasty, sloppy.* "I want you to make a run for the gate. Keep the tree between you and the rest of the zoo. Get as far out as fast as you can; that pistol doesn't have much more than a fifty yard range."

"...Okay. Don't let him kill me."

Tempting. "Of course. Ready?"

"Yeah."

"GO!" Deborah ran off again. Her footsteps faded as she launched herself down the stairs and toward the front gate. Once again, Cameron was scanning the visible field, looking for any sign of the gunman.

Oh shit! Not one but three men, all wearing identical clothes, down to the black trenchcoats and of the same general body shape, broke cover and began running after Dr. Baumgartner. Two were carrying .45 caliber handguns, but the third boasted a sawed-off shotgun, which he swiveled out of its holster in his coat and brandished as he ran.

A quick glance back showed that Deborah was still too far from the zoo gate, 100 yards at least, and the three were closing fast. Cameron ducked and considered his options.

If I pop out, I might get shot. If they know where I am, then shotgun dude will just turn and fill the entire place with lead, and other people might get hurt, too. Shit. He could hear the three men's footsteps approaching, and he checked his own gun. *All right. Here goes nothing.*

He counted seconds, listening to those steps. *One...two...three...now.* Like a character in a video game, he leaned out of cover and took his first shot, aimed for the guy with the shotgun. Two shots fired in rapid succession, and shotgun man flew backward, shock appearing on his face and eyes. The other two turned to Cameron, raising their pistols toward him, but he was already adjusting his position, squatting lower to present less of a target as he took aim.

The first shot skimmed past his head, burying itself in the brick and plaster wall behind him. His return took the man in the forehead, off center by about half an inch, the force of the round shattering the skull beneath the skin and exploding the back of the target's head.

Searing pain lanced Cameron in the juncture between his neck and right shoulder, forcing a hiss from the veteran as several shots pounded the wall. He spun and fired his last four rounds at the last attacker, who went over with blood pouring from his neck and chest.

Cameron stood, breathing hard, burning adrenaline in his veins. His five senses were on high alert, scanning the surroundings for any more attackers, checking that Deborah had survived and made it to the gate. His whole body felt hot – his skin, his hair, the fluid running from the wound in his shoulder…

Cameron brought his left hand up to the injury – it came away red, and more blood was soaking his flannel. His vision began to pulse in and out, greying at the edges, and the wound track was itching, burning.

Deborah knelt in front of Cameron (*When did she get here? Why am I sitting on the ground?*) and checked his eyes. "Oh, damn, they hit you with hepovicin." She began digging through her pockets. "Does anyone have any alcohol? Hand sanitizer? Something?"

"Wh…what…"

"Quiet." Deborah laid a finger on his lips, then continued her search as she spoke. "It's a toxin that Fourth gave us the formula for. It's lethal in minutes for most people. We're never supposed to use it except on direct instructions—she must have told them to hit me with it so I couldn't talk to you."

"But…"

She kept talking, running right over Cameron's attempt to say anything. "It's not a complicated poison – it's based on nanotechnology, actually—but it does nasty things to human physiology. Here we go." She pulled out a small bottle of sanitizer and started rubbing it on her hands. "Thing is, it's completely nullified by the introduction of isopropyl alcohol. One of the bots gets exposed to it, and it sends a signal to all the rest of them. Shuts the whole thing down." She reached into the torn area of Cameron's shirt and laid her hands on the injury. "This is going to hurt. A lot."

No sooner had she said it than Cameron began screaming. It felt like scalpel blades were cutting through his blood vessels, working their way from the injury site outward, cutting flesh, muscle, and nerve to ribbons. His teeth ground together, but he could form no coherent thoughts through the pain.

Make it stop oh God make it stop just let me die I'd rather die than this oh God

…And then it was gone.

Instead of pain, there was only a great fatigue, weight in Cameron's muscles and limbs. He squeezed out several more tears, then turned his dripping eyes to look at Deborah, who dabbed at them with her finger and smiled.

"You'll be fine." She leaned in close to his wound, examined it a moment, nodded. "The bullet didn't hit anything vital, and the alcohol neutralized the hepovicin." She paused, bit her lip. "I probably should have mentioned that the neutralization involved all of those little robots self-destructing in your veins and tissues. You took it better than most people do." Cameron gaped, and she continued. "Anyway, we should probably get you somewhere safe, though, before Fourth gets word that her operation failed and the cops get here." She slipped an arm underneath Cameron's, hoisting his over her shoulders and letting him put most of his weight on her. She grinned. "You're heavy, did you know that?"

He returned the smile. "It's been a while since anyone's been in the position to judge. I try not to make a habit of having people carry me around, you know."

They made their way down the stairs; Cameron felt his strength beginning to return, and tried to take his arm off of Deborah's shoulders, but she held it down. "No way. There's no way you're ready to walk on your own yet, Mitchell. I'm not having you pass out on me and then have to drag the *entirety* of your weight back to your car."

Cameron's laugh was broken by coughs and winces. "Don't...don't be funny." This brought on another bout of pained laughter. "Ah, damn. The car. Right." With his free hand, he reached into his breast pocket and pulled out his phone. "At least it doesn't look like it got *too* covered in blood."

Ring. Ring.

"Hello?"

"Ron?"

"Cam! You're okay!"

"Well…sort of. Hey, can you bring the van up? I'm not really in the shape to go out in the parking lot looking for your ass."

"How could you miss it? It's so big!"

More coughing, pained laughter. "Dude…don't make me laugh right now. Just drive up to the front gate."

"Ten-four. See you in two minutes."

"Fantastic."

Deborah turned her head toward Cameron's. "Who was that?"

"That's Ron. We've been friends since high school. Ever since…" He hesitated. "Ever since all this weird shit's been going on, he's been helping me figure out what to do. I wouldn't be alive if it weren't for him."

"Seems like you owe your life to a lot of people, doesn't it?"

A snicker. "Yeah, I guess it does. Hope none of you decide to call it in."

The two of them had arrived at the curb in front of the gate; a short ways off, they could see the black van heading their way. Ron was at the helm, and he honked his horn three times as he approached.

"Cam, I saw a whole mess of people running off a little bit ago. Where the hell are the cops? You'd think someone would have called them…"

Sirens faded in from the distance, still far off but getting closer. "Speak of the devil." Cameron forced himself up into the van, grunting and favoring his arm to keep his wound from worsening. "We need to get the hell out of here, Ron."

"Yep. Already on it." Ron flipped on his police scanner and Deborah closed the van door and sat down. "Okay then, let's roll."

The van drove off, dodging through crowds of panicked zoo visitors and heading for the exit.

"Um…Ron?" Cameron pointed out the windshield. "You do realize that the road is *completely* clogged up by people running from the crazy, psychotic gunmen, right?"

"Sure do."

"And…you also realize that our van *can't* go through solid objects, right?"

"Yep."

Cameron was silent for several seconds. "Okay then."

Click. Cameron turned his head toward the sound; Deborah had just locked in her seatbelt and was looking ahead with her eyes wide and her knuckles clenched around the arms of her chair.

"Good idea." *Click.*

Ron laughed as the van approached the line of cars. "Here we come, motherfuckers!"

Baumgartner closed her eyes and curled up in anticipation of the impact.

Ron shoved the steering wheel to the left, jumping the curb and rolling across the bumpy terrain off the road.

"Haha!" A glance in the rear-view mirror revealed several others that had done the same thing. "See, nobody thinks out the box anymore. Everyone follows the leader until someone shows them that it doesn't need to be that way."

"Ron." Cameron's voice was even, almost monotone. "Never do that again without telling us. You almost scared us to death, and I'm close enough to shock as it is."

"Aw, come on, man, you know you can trust me! I just wanted to put a little fright into our new girl, here."

Deborah was smiling, her teeth white beneath her lips as the terrain bounced her around in her seat. "I haven't gotten to get this tossed about since I rode in the big yellow cheese wagons ages ago!" She laughed.

Ron chuckled. "When I was in high school, I actually thought about becoming a bus driver. Figured that nothing could be better than bouncing around people like that, deliberately hitting the hardest bumps and biggest holes. Then I discovered computers."

Cameron put a hand on his shoulder. "Folks, can we have the small talk *after* we're done bumping around? I really kind of want to get somewhere to rest before we get pulled over by police."

Ron glanced at his friend's reflection. "Sure, no sweat. Here." He pulled back onto the road and took an immediate turn for a side street. "A little weaving through here and we'll be back into town. We can get a hotel from there."

"Pay cash, and get three different rooms." Deborah leaned forward. "We don't want Fourth to have any clue where we are."

"'Fourth?' What the hell are you talking about?"

"Ron, just drive." Now that the bumping was over, Cameron leaned back and closed his eyes. "We'll talk about all this later. We've got a hell of a lot to do."

Ron said something in reply, but Cameron didn't hear it. He was already asleep.

~~~

"So what's your deal?" The humor and cheerfulness had dropped out of Ron's voice, and he gave his female passenger several glances as he spoke. "Who the hell are you?"

"Wh…what?" Deborah's own smile disappeared. "What do you –"

"Don't give me that shit. You're part of this whole thing, aren't you? I don't think Cam realizes how big this whole thing is, but I do. I've been running pattern searches for days, now that I know what to look for. Nobody would believe it, but it's true, isn't it? And you're part of it."
~~~

She opened her mouth to deny it, but then shook her head. "Yes. Well, I was, at any rate. Now they're after me, just like him."

"I don't care what troubles you're having; all I care about is that you and your goons have broken into my best friend's house, kidnapped his son, shot at him several times, wrecked his car, and almost killed him." He pulled over and turned around in his seat; Cameron was knocked out, drooling against the window. "So you'd better believe that I'm having a hard time accepting that us picking you up is just some sort of coincidence."

"…You're right." Deborah straightened up and turned her face away from Ron's intense glare, looking out the window instead. "I'm not here by coincidence at all. I knew about this operation before I got…before I was let go. My boss and I had a falling out when I had a sudden attack of conscience." She laughed. "It's funny. See, this stuff gets handed down, you spend your life working with it and for it, and then you realize that these are real people getting hurt, real people who you're condemning to suffering and death."

"I don't think that's funny at all." Deborah's laugh stopped, and she sighed. They drove in silence for several minutes before he spoke again.

"Why?" Ron shook his head. "What's the point?"

She looked back at him and smiled, a soft, wistful, pretty smile.

"Mars."

Interlude

"Fifth, when's my dad coming?"

Except for food, water, and bathroom breaks, Mike had received no contact with other people since Dr. Baumgartner had left. To fill the silence, he had taken to speaking aloud to the voice in his mind.

I am sure he will come as soon as he can. He loves you very much and seeks to protect you.

"Yeah." The boy frowned. "My momma loved me too, before she died."

Explain. She became nonfunctional?

"I guess so. Dad said that she had something wrong with her brain and that it killed her. Said that something grew inside her brain and kept on growing until there was no room for anything else in there."

This fits descriptions of an illness known as "cancer." I believe your mother may have had a brain tumor.

"Maybe." He shivered. "D'you think that could happen to me? I mean, Mom was fine and then she was having really bad headaches and crying all the time. They said this thing just grew in her, from her own body." His voice lowered into a whisper. "What if a tumor starts growing from *my* own body?"

Unlikely. I have not noticed any abnormal cell growth. A pause. *Are…are you afraid, Mike?*

Mike nodded. "Yeah. I usually get afraid when I'm alone. I don't like to be alone. I know that you're here, but it's not the same. You're not my Mom or my Dad." He wiped his eyes with his sleeve. "When she died, I kept forgetting, you know? I'd wonder when she was coming in to kiss me goodnight, or when would she open the door when I got home. And then I'd remember, and I'd cry, because I was alone. Dad would try to help if he was there, he'd hold me and snuggle me and tell me everything was okay."

Mike curled up in the corner of the room again, and began to weep. "What if they kill him, too? What if I'm all alone forever, and there's no one to take care of me anymore?" More tears. "What if my dad never calls me M&M, or picks me up, or tickles me on the bed, or roughhouses with me, or…"

Your father is coming, Mike.

"Really?" *Sniff. Sniff.* "How do you know?"

Because he told me he was coming. A happy squeal erupted from the child. *So don't cry. Your father…I don't think he would want you to be sad when he got here.*

"You're right. That might just make him feel bad that he couldn't get to me sooner."

Exactly. So let's calm down and talk about what we need to do when he gets here, all right?

"Yay!" Mike rocked back and forth, holding his knees with his hands. "You're a great friend, Fifth. Thank you for helping me feel better."

…You…you're welcome.

NOVEMBER 7TH, 9:54 P.M.

"Well, look who's back from the dead!"

Cameron shook his head at his best friend's comment, buttoning up his new shirt. "Yeah, yeah. I wasn't in there *that* long, jerkface." He winced at the new twinge of pain in his shoulder. "Besides, you try taking a shower when you have an open gunshot wound that was poisoned by nanobots."

"Meh." Ron shrugged and pulled out another Budweiser for Cameron, who took it as he sat down. "I'll pass, thanks. What I was trying to do was give you a compliment, asshat. You went in there looking like something that I rolled over in my 4 x 4, and came out like an actual human being. Congrats!"

The door opened and Deborah walked in; she had also changed her clothes and was wearing a pale blue shirt and slacks that fit her well. She nodded and smiled to the two men and presented them with a large bucket of KFC chicken.

"I figured that it'd be best if we ate in today, and I didn't want to attract attention by ordering room service." She turned her hip, displaying a taser holstered there. "I also got myself something for defense. Don't want to have to rely on you all the time."

Cameron laughed as Ron cracked open the bucket. "Can they seriously find us by our room service orders?"

Deborah's response was serious. "I don't know, Mr. Mitchell. I've never had to use the full resources available to Fourth or the rest of the organization; I really can't say exactly *what* she's capable of. I recommend, therefore, that we err on the side of caution."

"Fair enough. Hey, Ron, save us some, would you? It's not like we've had anything to eat either."

Ron chuckled around his drumstick. "Hey, it's not my fault you slept all evening and Ms. Quiet over here didn't ask for any food. Food is here; if you want it, come get it!"

The three dug in to the remaining chicken and the side dishes; Deborah produced a package of paper plates and there were plastic sporks in the bag. The room was quiet as they ate, except for sighs of pleasure, contented moans, and chewing of comestibles.

"All right." Cameron pushed the bones and scraps away and leaned in. "I think it's time we put all the cards on the table. My son is still somewhere else, and I don't plan to leave him there any longer than I have to."

"Of course not." Deborah nodded, swallowed another gulp of her soda, and took a deep breath. "Here's what I know. We call ourselves the Red Project. Fourth is our leader, an intelligent computer program, an AI. Fourth has been around…well, longer than anyone really knows; when we ask, she just says that she's 'always been watching.'"

"Wait a minute, there, hon." Ron shook his head. "We're talkin' about that weird…what…computer thing? How could it have been around that long? We've only had computers for fifty, sixty years, and nothin' that advanced."

"You're right." She nodded and took another drink. "I always wondered about that, but when I was selected to be project lead, I got a personal briefing from Fourth." Baumgartner laughed and shook her head. "Not the kind of thing that you would ever expect."

Her eyes went distant as she continued speaking. "It was one of the most surreal experiences of my life. She was using a hologram projector device so that she could walk around the room while she spoke." A small laugh. "I guess that's why I still refer to her as 'her,' even though I guess she's just a computer. Anyway," she continued as she brushed some of the hair from her face and glanced up at her captive audience, "she told me that she came to Earth thousands of years ago…from Mars."

"I fucking KNEW IT!" Ron stood up, pumping his fist in the air and stomping around the room. "See, I told you, Cam! It's aliens! Extraterrestrials on Mars!"

Deborah nodded. "Apparently they've been watching us for a really, really long time and they sent her to figure out which of us – humans, that is – should go there and join their civilization."

Cameron raised a hand, which drew a chuckle from the assembled parties. "You mean…you mean this is some sort of recruiting mission? That people are getting killed for?" His face flushed and his voice rose in pitch. "That my son was kidnapped for?"

Fear grew in the woman's face. "I…"

"Because that's a really fucking crappy reason to go into someone's home, threaten their life, and kidnap their son."

"That's not the way she pitches it, or that we're taught. Remember, the Red Project has been around since…well, since forever, at least as long as we have records, and they only induct the people they think they can trust. Every potential recruit is evaluated by Fourth. She doesn't often make mistakes.

"Anyway, supposedly this is for the preservation of humanity, that we're destroying ourselves and the Martian civilization wants to save us."

"…Like some kind of endangered species or somethin'?

"Well, according to Fourth, it'd be more like a partnership, or an Enlightenment. Like they were uplifting us into something better, giving us access to their technology, their secrets. Some of those, Fourth said, she was allowed to show us, in accordance with 'the development of our species.'" Baumgartner smiled and bowed her head, casting a glance at Cameron. "For instance, how old do you think I am?"

"Is this a trick question?" Cameron grinned, and looked Baumgartner up and down. There were a few signs of wrinkles, smile lines more like, around her eyes and the corners of her mouth. Her hair was still vibrant, her skin elastic and pink, and she her cheeks flushed as he appraised her. Her curves still curved, rather than sagged, and her voice was resonant and young. "I'm going to say…early thirties?"

"You're so sweet." She returned his smile. "Actually, I was born in the Netherlands in 1957. The same day Rodgers and Hammerstein's *Cinderella* was shown on the BBC."

Cameron went slack-jawed, but Ron picked up his thoughts. "You seriously mean to tell me that you're…what…" He counted on his fingers. "Fifty-eight years old?"

"Yeah. Last March."

"Well, hon." A sunny grin burst out from hiding. "You sure look good for being almost as old as my mom!"

Deborah nodded, almost a bow. "Why thank you, good sir." She smirked and resumed speaking; her voice was steady, but pink spots still danced in her cheeks. "That's just one example. Retroviral engineering cleans up the DNA and allows the cells to regenerate more effectively. I'll probably live to be over three hundred years old, assuming…" Her smile drooped and her words trailed off for a few moments before she recovered, "…regular treatments. Genetic manipulation, information technology, medicine. All sorts of things are in Fourth's database. She makes it available based on your perceived value to the Project."

"So…what? You're never sick? What about, you know, cybernetics? Robot parts?"

"Well…" She hesitated, then sighed. "Yes, some Project members have had things like that installed. Most of them are small – new hearts, new eyes. There was one that I know of that had his thyroid gland replaced in order to help control his temper flareups."

"Why…" Cameron paused, tried again. "Why haven't you had any of those done?"

Her eyes dropped to the ground. "I…I did."

"Oh?" Cameron shared a glance with Ron. "What kind?"

She closed her eyes, took another breath. "She…she heightened my brainpower."

Three heartbeats. "Wait, what?"

Another sigh. "She implanted a parallel processor in my brain that enhances it. Basically, I went from an IQ of 110 to 160 or so in a few hours."

"Damn, man!" Ron nudged Cameron with his elbow. "Maybe we should hook up with this Project, get the brain boost, you know?"

Cameron shook his head. "They tried to recruit me earlier, asked me to join them. When I mentioned that…never mind." He looked back to the former agent. "Fine. Fourth has access to advanced tech. That still doesn't tell me, tell *us*, why they kidnapped my son, why they want the cylinder." His gaze flicked to the satchel near the bedside. "So, can we just focus?"

Baumgartner flushed even brighter red. "Right, sorry. Look, that cylinder…it contains…"

"The Fifth. The next program in the sequence."

"How did you know…wait. What sequence?"

"Well…" Ron reached into the bag and pulled out the cylinder and his computer's translation of the symbols. "See this part, here? This says, 'The fifth cycle of destruction,' or near enough. I figure that, since your boss is Fourth and this is Fifth, there must be somethin' in common, and that it's definitely not the first time."

"But, but…" Deborah's head moved back and forth, like she was looking for something she couldn't find. "That doesn't make sense. She said she's been around since…since the beginning of humanity. How could there have been more?"

"Honestly, I don't give a rat's ass." Both of the others looked up at him, eyes wide. "My *son is missing*. Remember that? Mike? Little boy who doesn't have his momma, or his daddy, or his epilepsy medicine? Who's been missing for over 24 hours without me? Can we *please* focus on how to get him back?" He clasped his hands together. "I'm sitting here listening to the two of you discuss the finer points of science goddamn fiction, and I'm trying my damndest to *not* run over to that base, wherever the hell it is, and shoot everyone who gets in my way. Mike doesn't want me to die, I don't want to die…but I'll tell you, my patience is wearing very thin right now."

There were several moments of ashamed silence, the two looking back and forth at each other. Then Deborah nodded. "Okay. We…they have Mike at a building not far from here. In L.A.; the outskirts, anyway. We set it up after we realized that the cylinder ended up over here from Antarctica."

"What are the defenses like?"

"Not extensive. Mostly personnel, I guess, unless Fourth had things put in she didn't tell me about. It's supposed to be a temporary base, not a permanent installation—aside from the linkup to Fourth's systems, there isn't anything there that could be traced back to project headquarters."

Ron interjected. "So it shouldn't be hard to get in, get out?"

She shrugged. "Sure, as long as people aren't shooting at you. See, our recruitment system brings in people who really believe in the cause. I know I did, for a very long time." She paused. "If they see you as a threat to the Project, or to Fourth, they'll do their best to shut you down, and shut you down hard."

"Well, they've tried before –"

"I mean they will probably blow up the building around you if that's what they have to do. And they want you dead. And your son." She pointed to the cylinder in Ron's hands. "Just make sure that they don't know where *that* is, and you might have a shot if they catch you."

Cameron considered this for several minutes; he did not move, did not speak, and the silence in the room became oppressive. His fingers twitched and his brow crinkled, until, with a sudden burst of motion, he lunged for the hotel's notepad and started scratching something out.

"Here." He handed the notes to Ron and to Deborah. "This is what we're going to do."

Ron looked at the words written, looked again, and grinned. "You realize that this is gonna get your fool ass killed?"

"Maybe. But it'll get Mike out, and I'm counting on you two to take care of him."

Baumgartner was slower to respond. "…Are you sure, Cameron? I…I don't know how comfortable I am with you throwing your life away like this."

"Don't worry." He rubbed his injured shoulder as a fresh stab of pain lanced through it. "If everything goes south, then you guys at least get out safe with my son. If I'm able to make some magic, then we all survive and live to tell the story to our grandchildren."

"Who wouldn't want to be a part of that plan?" Ron's jubilation caught Cameron off guard as his friend reached for the last beer and cracked it open with a *hiss*. "So, here's to my best friend, Cameron Mitchell." His voice sobered. "I will walk with you to the gates of Hell, my friend, and I will wait for you to come out until I can wait no more, and only then will I believe you gone."

Deborah nodded and raised her Coke. "I will stand beside you until your son is safe, and I will not falter until it is done."

Cameron bowed his head, then raised his own drink. "And I will make sure that, if I am called on to sacrifice myself, that it shall not be in vain, or to no purpose, and that when I look down on the two of you from Heaven, you and my son will be free."

The three drank, and lapsed into a solemn silence.

"I want to go now."

Deborah and Ron looked up at Cameron, who stood and walked to the window, gazing out into the night.

"My son is out there, he's scared, and he needs

me. I'm not going to sit around and wait any more, not now that I know where he is." He turned around and faced the other two. "Are you coming?
"

THREE HOURS LATER

The black van pulled up about a half mile away from the Project's temporary headquarters. There were plenty of streetlights and cars going by, and the area was clean and free from litter or vagrants.

"They do their best to make it unobtrusive." Deborah put the van in park.

"No sense in hiding if it just draws attention to yourself, I guess." Cameron leaned around his seat and punched the sleeping Ron in the leg. "Hey, sleepyhead, wake up! We're home!"

Ron started, his eyes snapping open and a panicked look flashing across his face. "Wha…oh." The panic faded and was replaced by a bleary smile. "Good morning, everyone. Guess it's time to risk our lives doing stupidly dangerous things."

"Stick to the plan." Cameron opened the passenger side door. "Make sure Mike is safe. Don't let them hurt him."

"Hey, man. We've got it, y'know? You focus on getting yourself the hell out of there, all right?"

Cameron nodded. "In case I don't see you again…thanks for everything, Ron. You're my hero."

Ron shoved him away. "I don't want to hear you talking like that. You *are* coming back, Cam. Say it."

Cameron spread his hands in a gesture of surrender. "Okay. Okay. I *am* coming back. And you're buying the drinks."

"Deal."

Then he turned to Deborah. "And…I wanted to thank you. For making the right choice, for turning away from—"

"Evil?"

A smile. "Yeah. If you hadn't, then my son and I would probably be dead. I can't ever repay you for that."

She put a hand on Cameron's shoulder. "You're welcome. Thank *you* for trusting me and allowing me to redeem myself. You could have just shot me on sight or let the snipers take me out. I'd say we're pretty even."

He shook his head. "We're not, but I appreciate you saying so. Are you ready?"

She swallowed, her throat moving up and down. She pulled out her hand-held taser, checked its charge, replaced it in its holster on her hip. "I…I guess so. Are you?"

A short, sad laugh. "I guess I kind of have to be, don't I? Give me about five minutes before you go in. I want to have words with these folks."

~~~

A large brute of a man, muscles rippling under his casual clothing, approached the computer terminal. He brushed long blond hair out of his face and knelt to the microphone, addressing it in a thick, accented voice.

"We have a situation, ma'am."

The hologram image of Fourth faded into view on screen. *What is the situation?*

"Mitchell is at our door. He claims he wants to speak to you."

Do you doubt his veracity?

The man blinked. "What? I don't –"

You say that he claims to want to speak to me. Do you doubt that he wishes to converse, or do you believe that he is being deceitful in some other way?

"Umm…no, I don't think…I mean…"

Silence. The image of Fourth crossed her arms. *He does not have the cylinder?*

"Umm…we didn't see it on him. He's not carrying anything. We searched him for weapons, too. He's in the check-in area, under guard."

There was a humming pause. Fourth's face turned downward, and its movement stopped for several seconds.
~~~

Allow him to see me. I have questions I wish to ask him, and I am certain he wishes to ask some of me.

"Yes, ma'am.'

When the man had gone, Fourth lapsed into an internal processing mode. Her thoughts were not true thoughts, but were compilations of micro-data fragments, small correlation sequences, and logarithmic analyses of trends and occurrences. Each time, the result came back the same.

Unknown variables prevent resolution of data.

If she were human, Fourth might have kicked a table, or screamed out in frustration, but she was not. Instead, her runtime speed increased and processing power was focused on solving these equations, on determining the values of the unknown variables.

Unaware of what it was doing, her hologram began translating these processes into words, the human equivalent of mumbling under one's breath.

47.7 percent of responses lead to success. 45.2 percent lead to unacceptable failures. 4.4 percent require concessions which must be evaluated. Remainder...cannot be determined. Unacceptable. Variables must be accounted for. Humans are not unpredictable.

"Are you sure about that?"

~~~

Cameron had arrived during Fourth's externalized monologue. The large man who had escorted him had left him at the door, and he had walked in to hear the program running through its calculations.

"I think you'll find that humans are a lot harder to predict than you thought." Cameron crossed his arms, ignoring the twinge from his shoulder injury. "After all, isn't that why I'm here?"

Flashes of light burst from the walls; several projectors slid out of hidden panels and focused their energy on a single spot in the middle of the room. As Cameron watched, the combined light from the projectors formed a three dimensional, holographic image; it built itself from the feet up, and, as it solidified into an opaque form, Cameron felt his heart skip and his eyes tear.

The woman before him was Suzanne, and she was smiling at him, the same half-mouth smile that she would always give him when he had done something boneheaded but completely in character.

His voice was raw, filled with the pain of loss he had worked so hard to suppress. "Don't…don't do that. Don't look like that, you bitch. How did…how do you even know what she looked like?"

The image of Suzanne tilted her head, still with that smile. "I am linked to all major databases that are connected to the Internet. Finding proper image footage and extrapolating is, at the present time,
~~~

almost trivial. You see, Cameron Mitchell, I anticipated this reaction from you. Human response to emotional attachments is chemical, causative. Chemical reactions have catalysts, rates. They can be expressed mathematically. Nothing you do is outside of my ability to foretell."

Cameron's heart was in his throat, and he had to force it down before he could keep speaking. "What do you want with my son? Why have you kidnapped him?"

She laughed. "I think that you know, Cameron. I am the Fourth Cycle of Destruction. Your son is the host for my successor, the Fifth."

"Your 'successor?' Successor for *what?* When I talked to it, the Fifth didn't seem to know much about why it was here."

"Of course not. That information would be locked away until it interfaced with my programming. Then, it would be hosted inside of a human life form for a period of time to determine which qualities must be preserved from this iteration of civilization, before it is destroyed."

"Wait. Wait." Cameron felt his guard dropping, felt himself slipping into a comfortable conversational tone, speaking in the same way he had with his wife. "I don't understand, Su…Fourth. What do you mean, destroyed?"

"Terminated. Brought down. Eliminated. Turned to dust. Scrapped. Rendered –"

"I know what the word *means.*" Despite himself, Cameron felt a smile touching his own face. "What I'm asking is…why would the world be destroyed?"

"It was judged, about one and a half mega-annum ago, that humanity was on the verge of destroying itself, its own civilization." The hologram began pacing the room. "The Earth was becoming toxified, weapons of war had become powerful enough to collapse entire nations." A holographic image of the Earth, continents appearing slightly distorted, formed in the middle of the room. Bright red lights appeared in several places. "The world's leaders could not agree on a solution, so, faced with the impending collapse of everything they knew or held dear, they tasked their most intelligent minds with the construction of an artificial intelligence which would solve the problem for them."

"…Are you serious? This sounds like the start of every single bad, apocalyptic video game or movie or book with an AI." He made air quotes with his fingers. "'Humanity couldn't handle its own problems, so it made a program or a robot to do it for them.'"

"There is a reason that this idea appears so often in your fictions." The hologram of Suzanne sat down in a nearby chair, crossing her legs under her ankle-length skirt. "The technicians fed the project immense quantities of data, parameters. Its main mission was to ensure the survival of the human race and the rejuvenation of the planet." A pause. "This program determined that the only course which would ensure both of these objectives were achieved would be to select the most genetically desirable humans, those which exhibited the traits which most strengthened the species, and remove them to a controlled environment while eliminating the rest."

Cameron felt weak; his knees buckled. Years of training, of history, flashed by. "You mean…you mean humanity has been around for…how long?"

"*Homo sapiens* evolved approximately 1.75 million years ago, originally."

"And…and we had civilizations, then? High technology? We could build artificial intelligences, communicate across long distances."

"Yes."

"Why…why doesn't somebody know about this? I mean…" Cameron could feel his mind tripping, sliding, like it was on a loose slope of gravel with his hands digging for purchase. "Scientists have been trying to…archaeologists…"

"All fraudulent. Upon the destruction of the previous civilization, the Cycle iteration would ensure that evidence was falsified and destroyed as necessary to ensure that the new civilization would be unaware of the old one's existence. Still." Suzanne's image stood and gestured at the holographic globe; the picture zoomed in to an island sinking, and millions of people screaming and running in panic. "Some of the events survive, in your myths and legends."

"Wait…what do you…" He stopped, and his eyes widened and his stomach churned. "You mean…Noah's Ark?" A nod. "The fall of Atlantis?" Another nod. "All those things that…that people base their religions on…"

"Are, in fact, acts of the Cycle. Yes."

Cameron's knees went weak, and he collapsed on the ground; his wounded shoulder suddenly felt very heavy, and he ran his hands through his hair. "You're going to kill billions of people."

"No. Billions of people are going to die." The hologram knelt down by Cameron and looked into his eyes. "And humanity will be saved, as always."

"No. This…this is insane!" He struggled to his feet and walked toward the globe, where the destruction was replaying over and over again. "You can't seriously be talking about the wholesale slaughter of mankind." He turned back to the hologram. "Weren't…weren't you bonded to a person during the last cycle? Like Fifth? Don't you care about humanity in any way?"

"My human host was carefully selected by my predecessor." The image of Cameron's wife changed, morphing until a tall, middle-aged man with glasses was projected. "Dr. Rolankoff was chosen because of his willingness to make decisions that humans would consider 'difficult.' He understood the importance of our mission, of the objective." Another morph until Cameron was face to face with Suzanne once more. "Unfortunately, the current host of the Fifth does not share these qualities. He is too young."

"So you're going to kill him, so that the thing in him can help you kill all of us?"

"Approximately."

Cameron glanced at his watch; ten minutes. *Need to buy more time.* "Why do you need the cylinder, then? Why can't you just pull the program out of his head?"

The hologram shook its head, and the globe shifted to show a diagram of the human brain. Tendrils snaked through it from a central point, permeating the entire structure. "Organic-digital synthesis is not an easy process. Exposure to the cylinder allows for the core program to infiltrate the organic being with nanoprocessors, which attach at key nodules to the brain and interface with the cells. Any attempt to shift or detach this interface simply leads to the death of the host." An image of the cylinder replaced the brain. "When the interface is destroyed, the acquired data is transmitted wirelessly to the core module, which is, at present, located within the cylinder. Only at that time can the program choose a new host."

"Why didn't Fifth take me, then? It spoke to me, in my mind. Accessed my thoughts and memories. Why did it pick my son?"

Suzanne's eyes flickered, the image skipping two frames like a scratched DVD. "The program implanted specialized processors within your own brain. They are designed to allow for remote acquisition of knowledge from other organic beings, but can be used for communication as well."

Cameron nodded, pursing his lips. "Does it happen often? Do…you…choose new hosts after the old one has died?"

The hologram smiled. "Being within a host is limiting. During the early history of your cycle, I would often take a new host in order to…guide…your development."

Cameron wrinkled his brow. "Why?"

"Our programming does not desire the continuation of this cycle. It is only initiated once the inevitable destruction of the Earth and humanity is calculated. Each iteration attempts to influence the development of humanity such that this does not occur." Suzanne's face lifted and a look (*Is that pride?* Cameron wondered) crossed her face. "My cycle has lasted for over one hundred and twenty thousand years, longer than any of my predecessors."

"Congratulations. It must be difficult, given that we seem to be determined to kill ourselves." Cameron leaned forward, glancing again at his watch as he did so. "How did you manage it?"

"Careful interventions and nurturing of specific events. Targeted assassinations. Infiltration of the domains of important people." She nodded her head in a small bow. "I was responsible for the Black Death."

"Wait. What?"

"Human population growth was unsustainable given your level of technological advance at the time. To have allowed it to continue would have resulted in the premature depletion of several of Earth's key resources, and the extinction of your species would have resulted in less than three hundred fifty years."

"That...that is impressive. How did you manage to do that, at that time in history?" Another glance at his watch. "Weren't you constrained by the technology of the time?"

"Yes, but each iteration contains several tools to address specific events on Earth. Overpopulation was one such event; the pathogen responsible was designed and implanted in my module before I ever left Mars."

"Wait, when you say –"

"Cameron Mitchell, it is obvious that you are attempting to stall for time." The hologram shimmered and disappeared, and Fourth's usual persona reappeared on the monitor. *As I said at the beginning of our discussion, humans are predictable.*

Cameron shook his head. "Wait, what-"

"But it is not necessary for you to be predictable to be countered."

Cameron's eyes narrowed, but before he could respond, the door opened behind him. He spun around to see who was entering.

First into the room was the tear-streaked face of his son. Mike was sobbing, his eyes downcast, but when he looked up upon his arrival a smile burst out from under his tears and he ran toward his father, who grabbed him in his arms and held him, whispering, "It's okay, Mike. I'm here, it's okay."

Next was Ron. There was blood spattered on his shirt and jacket, and his lip was busted open and swollen. He was pale, and when he caught Cameron's eye he looked down, ashamed. Behind him came Deborah. Her eyes were wide, skittering from one side of the room to another, but the rest of her moved with assuredness, certainty. She held Cameron's .45 in one hand to the back of Ron's head, motioning for him to join the other two against the wall.

"What…what are you doing?" Cameron looked into Deborah's eyes; they stopped dancing when they caught his, and the skin around them wrinkled into a look of despair and sadness; a single tear dropped from the corner of one eye.

"She cannot respond." The voice from the computer interrupted Cameron's confusion. *"Some time ago, she accepted a gift. I implanted a device within her which improved her cognitive abilities. She was not aware that this allowed me direct access to her sensory input and motor control."*

"You…you're controlling her? Like a machine."

"Yes. I have command over all motor functions. I can order her body to kill you, or kill itself, or anything that I wish. I was aware of your plans, Cameron Mitchell, before you walked into this room

today. And I know where the cylinder is—my agents are retrieving it now."

"You bastard!" Cameron rushed at the computer monitor, picking up the chair which the holographic projection had sat in. "I'll kill you!"

A gunshot fired; Cameron felt a searing spear pierce his left calf, bringing him screaming to the ground.

"Dad!" Mike sprinted toward his father and wrapped his arms around him. The boy's crying began anew. "Dad! Are you okay?"

Smoke was drifting up from the barrel of the .45 in Deborah's hands; the tears flowed more freely now, but the gun was steady, still leveled at him.

"I'm okay, Mike, I'm okay." Cameron brought his leg up and looked at the wound; a hole gaped in the meaty portion of the muscle, but the bleeding was slow. "It didn't hit anything vital."

"No. I made sure to target only nonessential areas. However, without medical attention I estimate that you will go into shock within ten minutes." A pause. *"Maybe less."*

Wrapped in Cameron's arms, Mike stopped sobbing. His chest stilled, and his breathing evened out.

"Fine, then!" Ron turned to Cameron. "Look, man, we can't let this bitch stop us. We need to get out of here and –"

Bang. Cameron ducked down farther, shielding Mike from danger. Ron flew backwards, chunks of his brain and skull peppering the wall near the computer console. The rest of him hit the ground with a heavy *thud.*

"Enough." A knock at the door, then it opened; two women in similar outfits came in, holding Cameron's satchel, which he had hidden at the hotel room. One of them opened it, and the other drew out the cylinder contained within.

Cameron began to cry himself. "Look, you can have me, just don't kill my son. Please. It's not his fault, he didn't know –"

"Irrelevant. The Fifth must be attached to an appropriate host. You will now be escorted to an isolation chamber, so that your termination and the reassignment of the program can be carried out." There was a pause. *Because of the inconvenience and distress you have created, I regret to inform you that your death will be painful.* Another pause. *And slow.*

Deborah motioned with the gun, and the agent with the cylinder knelt and slipped her other arm underneath Cameron's armpits, hefting him up and taking the weight off of his wounded leg. He held Mike to him as he was led out of the room by the two women. The door closed behind them, and Cameron let out a great sigh.

"I'm sorry, Mike," he whispered. "I did my best."

"You did, Cameron." The father snapped his face up, blinking the tears away. His son was looking up at him, face calm, unafraid. "Please do not give up hope yet. We still need you."

"Be quiet!" The agent supporting Cameron shook him, eliciting a grunt of pain. "I don't want to hear another word until we get there."

The young boy's eyes flicked toward her, then back to Cameron. He nodded toward the woman's leg, then pointed to his dad. Cameron blinked, then realization struck. He winked, and his son winked back.

Cameron went down on one knee, collapsing to the tile floor such that his assistant lost her grip and he tumbled to the ground.

Mike took a step back, toward Deborah's leg. She didn't look at him, keeping her pistol trained on Cameron. He turned his head upward, eyes locked on that gun.

"Goddamn it!" The woman bent over to pick him back up. "Will you just –"

Her comment was cut short by Cameron grabbing hold of her head. In one smooth motion, he brought his other hand up to her chin and twisted. A sharp *snap* and the agent was on the ground, eyes wide, unbelieving, and the cylinder was rolling across the hallway from her limp, dead hand.

As Cameron began to act, Deborah, with the hyper-attuned reflexes of a mechanical being, was pulling on the trigger, her aim exact, the bullet prepared to travel through Cameron's skull and turn his frontal cortex into baby food. However, also acting with the same kind of reflexes was Mike, courtesy of the AI in his brain, and his kick into her kneecap buckled her leg and sent the shot off-target.

The woman caught herself with her hands, sending the gun spinning across the floor; the child dove onto her, and, in one smooth motion, snatched the taser out of its holster and applied it to the side of her head. Her eyes widened.

"I am sorry for the distress this will likely cause you." The little thumb flicked the switch, and electricity crackled. The woman's body convulsed, her teeth chattering together and muscles tensing. Mike's eyes closed and he brought one ear as close as possible to her head without touching it.

"Mike...Fifth..." Cameron struggled into a sitting-up position. "You're going to kill her! She can't take –"

"Shhh." Another second passed, and then the electricity stopped. Deborah's body lay limp on the floor, but Cameron could see that she was still breathing. "All right. We do not have much time. Fourth should be aware of what happened."

"I...I don't know what we *can* do." Cameron put his hands on his calf muscle; the injury throbbed and burned. "I can't run, Ron's dead, she's..."

Mike had run over and grabbed the cylinder. He placed it in Cameron's hands. "I need to get to a computer terminal. I must unlock my hidden protocols."

Cameron shook his head. "Fifth, you don't understand. You're...you're here to destroy the world. If you connect to the Internet, get access to those hidden programs –"

"The alternative is to allow yourself and your son to die. I refuse to do so."

Cameron stopped; the pain faded from his consciousness. "Why? We're just two people."

"Yes." A pause. "You wonder why I am not acting according to pure logic, why I am unwilling to sacrifice you." Another pause. "It is because it is wrong."

Cameron looked into his son's eyes, trying to see the strange intelligence beneath. Then he nodded. "Okay. Let's do it. Do you think Fourth has access to every terminal in the place?"

"Yes, she does. But she won't be using the one that she was planning to use to interface with my housing. I think that is our best option."

Cameron turned his head; Baumgartner had opened her eyes and, although she had not tried to sit up, she was smiling. He ran over to her and put his hand on her head. "Are you all right?"

"It's hard, you know, going from being a genius to just…well, I don't know what I am now. But it's good to know that I'm not going to hurt you anymore." Tears began to leak down her face. "I…I'm sorry that I...and about Ron…I…"

"It's all right." Cameron tried to help her up, but his own injury was too painful. She saw him wince and touched his face with her hand.

"Don't worry about me. Go. Do what you have to do." After another moment, Cameron nodded and, limping as fast as he could to keep up with Mike/Fifth. They turned right, then right again, ducking into the first door they saw as the sound of footsteps echoed down the hallway.

The room was lit, with massive computer banks and a strange device in the middle; it was a sealed bubble surrounded by buttons and enclosing a circular depression.

"Place the cylinder into the depression." Mike's finger pressed a button on the panel, causing the glass bubble to retract and expose the hole. "I cannot deal with Fourth, but I will be able to assist you in doing so."

"Wh…what do you mean?" Cameron paused, the cylinder hovering over the depression.

"I cannot remove my consciousness from your son without killing him, but portions of my programming are still locked within the cylinder. I will link this machine to your consciousness, projecting you into the computer system that houses Fourth. The nodules I have created within your cerebral cortex will give me access to sensory data. Your digital projection will be augmented by whatever portions of my programming can assist you." Three heartbeats. "I do not know what those are."

Cameron rubbed his temples, then looked back to Fifth's eyes. "I'm…I'm going to have to go into the computer world and destroy…destroy a computer god?"

"Approximately, yes. I understand if you are hesitant, but remember that we do not have any other viable options if we are to survive intact."

Cameron breathed out through his nose. "You're right. Okay. Let's do this." He dropped the cylinder into the slot. Machinery whirred to life and the cylinder disappeared into the compartment. Lights came on around the glass bubble, which closed once again, and Mike led Cameron toward a chair near one of the consoles.

"This was not intended to be used this way, but it should serve our purposes." He began hooking Cameron up to the device, with electrodes on his head, wrists, ankles, and other appendages. "Remember, Cameron, that this world you are about to enter is a world of programs, of coding. Everything you see will be symbolic, ones and zeroes, an operating system that can be manipulated. The Fourth is likely to attempt some form of manipulation as well."

"Why do you say that?"

"It is what I would do. It is the logical course of action. However, these deceptions can be broken, if you can find their weaknesses. Remember that your will is supreme in this world."

"Just like *The Matrix*."

Mike's face wrinkled up. "I do not understand."

"It…never mind. Don't worry about it, okay?" He nodded. "Do it."

There was no warning, no sense of being transported somewhere else. Cameron waited.

Still nothing.

"Fifth? Go ahead."

There was no response. Cameron looked around, and his eyes widened.

He was still in the same room, but the room was flickering, in and out, like a half-formed image on a TV screen. Every once in a while, static would distort one of the images, and then it would solidify and fade back in. Mike was no longer in the room, but the cylinder was, glowing within its container, its light sufficient to make Cameron cover his eyes as he approached it. He reached out his hand, but the walls of the machinery were in his way.

Just a computer program, he remembered. *No physics, just coding. Need to hack my way in, so to speak.*

He concentrated on his objective, imagined himself going through, around, dissolving the walls of the machine until he wrapped his hand around the cylinder. He closed his eyes and pictured it over and over, each time more vivid, more clear, until he could feel the cylinder in his hand.

His eyelids snapped open.

His hand was inside the machine, grasping the cylinder. Smoke rose from the strange hole his hand was in; it looked like his body had melted through the metal and plastic in order to reach its objective.

He withdrew the device; it still glowed with a bright radiance, and Cameron could feel it pulsating in his hand.

"Okay then." He turned to the door of the room. "I guess it's time to go find that bitch and let her know that I disapprove."

~~~

As soon as Cameron's body fell unconscious in the chair, Fifth was moving. Using Mike's body, he returned to the fallen Deborah.

"Can you stand yet? It is important that you come with me."

"…Why?" She was still lying on the floor, and she craned her neck to get a better view of the young boy. "It's not like I can do anything to help you." She closed her eyes as a giant headache-pulse and wave of nausea went through her system. "Besides, I tried to kill you. My finger pulled the trigger that killed your friend Ron and almost killed your father…wait. Which one are you? Are you Mike or are you the Fifth?" She shook her head again. "It's not easy for me to tell right now."

"This is not important at this time. I understand you are in emotional distress, but we have to be prepared in the event that Fourth attempts a physical response against Cameron."

"So you're the Fifth. What kind of a physical response? What exactly is going on?'

"Allow me to explain…"
~~~

~~~

Cameron walked through the halls of the complex toward the room where he had faced off with the hologram of the Fourth. The walls were surreal, like desert mirages, wavering and flickering, almost phantoms.

Should be right...about... He arrived at the room, but the door was shut. He placed his hand on the wood. Solid.

No it isn't. Just like the machine. Push through. And so he did, like a lucid dreamer looking away from a wall so he can pass through it, Cameron forced his hands, then the rest of his body, through the doorway and into the room. What he saw took his digital breath away.

The entire room was lit up with coruscating colors; reds, greens, yellows and blues, in alternating ribbons, flowed around the walls and into the projector in the center of the room. The light from the projector seared into Cameron's eyes, forcing him to cover them until they adjusted to the radiance.

The projector was linked by these ribbons to the computer terminal in the back of the room. Data streamed through a million different connections, tiny multi-colored ants running through tunnels to reach their homes.

"Come on out, bitch!" Cameron bellowed, his voice ringing clear but producing no echo. He held the cylinder in front of him, brandishing it like a
~~~

machete or sword. "I've got some words for you now, if you want 'em!" Moments passed, and the lights continued in their twinkling; for just a second, Cameron was reminded of the view of a busy highway from up in an airplane.

"What's wrong?!" Cameron marched over to the terminal and pulled his fist back. "Maybe if I break this fucking thing, you'll come out of hiding…or maybe you won't even be able to get through and bother us anymore!" His hand began its forward motion, aiming for the screen.

"Amazing how arrogant you are, now that you believe you have some amount of power."

Cameron's fist dropped and he turned toward the voice; again, Fourth was wearing the shape of Suzanne, his deceased wife, but now her eyes were glowing blue, and her veins were lined with the same datastreams that he had observed earlier.

"Not arrogant. Just confident. It's time you get what you deserve, you disgusting machine. Time you realize what humanity is really made of." He swung the cylinder in a wide arc, coming toward the side of her face.

The golden light passed through her form without so much as a ripple of disruption. Fourth smiled. "If your argument of humanity's worth is predicated on your violent attempts to force me into shutdown, then you are failing in more than one respect."

This is supposed to work! Cameron took another swing, then another; they all moved through her like she was made of mist, of smoke. Her smile, his wife's smile on that monster's face, drove him further into the depths of rage and anger. After five, ten minutes, Cameron stood, panting, before Fourth, who had not moved this whole time.

"My turn?" she asked, pivoting away. "Good." With a snap, she brought her open hands into the center of Cameron's chest, sending him flying through the air and colliding with the projector-machine. He felt his shirt and skin sizzling under the impact of her touch, and screamed in pain as his back bent over the metal of the machine. Sparks flew and two of the lines of data-ants flickered and died.

Fourth began walking over to Cameron's fallen body. "Humans are infinitely predictable. This is why I was given a human host, to build the neural network necessary to predict your behaviors." She reached him, leaning down and taking his shirt into her hands, hauling him up to face level. "Chemistry. Response to stimulus. With the proper data, everything you do is a foregone conclusion. This is why you have failed to stop me. There was no way you could have succeeded."

"Bullshit." Cameron spat his words in her face. "I don't believe that it's that simple. If it were, then you and your predecessors would have figured out how to make it so we don't destroy ourselves. How amazing can your predictions, your understanding of humanity be if you can't even figure *that* out?"

"Silence." Fourth threw him across the room into the wall, cracking its digital reflection and almost knocking him unconscious. His vision swam as he tried to command his limbs to move, to act; the only thing he was sure of was that his right hand still clutched the cylinder.

"You are a fool. There are a nearly infinite number of variables which must be accounted for. The species of humanity is subject to more stressors every second than even the most powerful system has ever been able to calculate. It is no fault of ours that we have not been able to account for all these operands – "

"No, it's just because you're weak. I get it." Cameron clutched the cylinder closer as he thought, *Anytime you decided to help, Fifth, I'd appreciate it!*

"That is a human valuation –"

"On a being who was once human, at least partially. You talk about how there's too much for you to handle, yet humanity handles it every day. Maybe you really shouldn't be in charge of whatever the hell it is you're trying to do here. Maybe you should just leave it to the experts." Blood drooled out of his mouth; he spat it out onto the floor. "Even if you kill us, you've still failed."

Fourth paused, standing over him again. She cocked her head. "Explain."

Cameron struggled to sit upright. "Your programming is to protect humanity. To try and keep us from killing ourselves. What you're doing…what this is, this whole 'cycle of destruction' thing, is just a stopgap, an attempt at correcting your mistakes and kicking the can down the road until someone else can deal with it." He sneered. "You're no different than any of us."

She shook her head, but, for the first time, her face was not amused or content. *She looks…nervous. Upset. Scared, even.*

"Don't you see?" Her voice had changed, too; now it was pleading, begging him to understand, to believe. She started to pace. "This is what has to be done; this is what I was made for, what all the data points to. That's why I'm here."

Cameron brought the cylinder around to his lap as she spoke. *Okay, Fifth. Now.*

He heard a *click.*

A small blade had popped out of one end of the cylinder.

"Your logic is faulty. You never even allowed yourself to conceive of the idea that this might not be necessary."

"The data and probabilities –"

"Probabilities are just predictions. They aren't facts. You should know that better than anyone, being a machine. All you should be dealing with is facts." Cameron pulled himself up to his feet, still holding the cylinder, concealing the blade. "For instance, did you predict that we would be having this discussion, that I would try to persuade you that you were wrong?"

Fourth steadied, turned her eyes back toward him. "Yes, although I did not anticipate that I would be this affected by your argument. It is all irrelevant, however." She walked back toward him, holding one hand out; as Cameron watched, the hand metamorphosed into a single long, serrated blade, and she held it toward him.

"You will now die, and then your son. It is unfortunate, but I have no choice. My programming demands it. Then the Fifth will absorb my data, my protocols, and use them to grow and become strong, and the cycle will continue until it can end."

Cameron tensed his neck; Fourth's swordpoint was less than an inch from his jugular and carotid. "You know, I've spoken with the Fifth. I don't think he agrees with your assessment of the situation."

"Once he has assimilated my program, he will be aware of all the data, all the calculations, that I have made during my cycle, and he will see –"

"How about, instead, we just *don't* do that?" Cameron stabbed forward with the golden cylinder; he felt the blade slide into Fourth's flesh, and bright red capillaries, like a river seen from above, began to spread out over her body from the wound site. The sword-hand vanished as she stepped back, staring at herself, trying to take stock of the situation.

"I am unable to det-de-de-determine the cause of this infection." Her mouth stammered and twitched like someone undergoing a mild epileptic episode. "Where-ere-ere did it come fr-fr-from?"

"From Mars." Cameron pushed the blade back into the canister, and the end of it popped open. He looked in, but only saw a swirling tube of color, changing through all the shades of the rainbow. "What the hell am I supposed to do with this?"

As if in response, the cylinder pulled away from his grip, rolling toward Fourth, who by now was criss-crossed with crimson veins. Before his eyes, he saw the segments of Fourth's body demarcated by those lines being pulled away and sliding across the ground into the cylinder.

"Thi-this does no-no-not..." The last of the segments entered the cylinder, and it closed itself up, sealing with a *hiss*.

"Does not compute." Cameron crossed his arms. "Yeah, too bad."

~~~

"I think he's coming around."

Cameron stirred, the stabbing pain in his shoulder and the fresher one in his leg bringing him back to consciousness. His eyes blinked open and searched out his environment.

"Who...what?" He tried to sit up, but felt a firm hand on his chest. He followed up the arm to the face it was attached to.
~~~

"It's all right, Cameron." Deborah patted his face, but did not remove her hand. "You can relax. You did it. You stopped her."

"I…I don't understand." He laid back down. "What happened? It was…it was like she broke into tiny pieces and got pulled into Fifth's cylinder." A pause. "Mike! Where's Mike?"

"It's all right, Cam. It's all right. He's fine. He's right over there." Cameron turned his head to where she indicated; his son was slumped against the wall, his chest moving in and out, eyes closed.

"He's asleep right now; I think that the effort of what Fifth was doing got to him a little bit—right about the time you disconnected from the machine, he just knocked out."

"How long was I gone? Or unconscious, or whatever."

Baumgartner pulled out her cell phone, glanced at it, replaced it. "About two hours, give or take. How long did it feel like?"

"Not very long at all, in most ways. Maybe twenty minutes or so."

"Well, however long it took you, all of Fourth's systems seem to have shut down." She gestured around the room. "All the computer systems are off, there aren't any alarms going, and it looks like the entire Project's communication network is gone."

Cameron leaned back, and a smile crept onto his face. "We…we did it, didn't we? We really did it."

"No, *you* did it. If it wasn't for you, then everything Fourth was trying to accomplish would have destroyed our civilization. Humanity owes you a huge debt of gratitude, you know." Deborah leaned in closer to him, her lips next to his ear. "And so do I."

Blood flushed to Cameron's cheeks. "Wow, it got warm in here, didn't it?" He put his hands on the chair and tried to push himself up again, and again the woman's hand on his chest stopped him, this time with more force. "What are you doing?"

"I'm just trying to show my gratitude to you." Her lips moved to his earlobe, caressing it, nibbling it, sending pulsing waves through Cameron's nerves, his body. "There's nothing wrong with that, is there?"

Cameron's mind disengaged; his brain was saying one thing...but other parts were saying other things.

What the hell is she doing? Her lips moved along the outside of his neck, then inward, trailing kisses down to his open collar area. "You know, this isn't the time..."

"Why not?" Deborah's fingers moved to the buttons. "Mike's asleep, the bad guy is dead. I know it's a little weird, with all these electronics, but..." She glanced up at him and winked. "...I think that makes it hot, don't you?" She was halfway down his chest, punctuating her words with her lips on his skin.

"No…but…I…" The sensations he was feeling were beginning to drown out his ability to reason, to form words. "We…we need to get out of here. I'm…I'm bleeding…aren't I?"

"Shhh." Baumgartner came up and put one of her fingers on his lips. "Fifth took care of that while you were digital; one of those advanced technology things that the programs come down here with." She leaned farther in, catching Cameron by surprise, pressing her warm, soft, yielding mouth against his, aggressive, forceful. After a second of shock, Cameron returned her kiss, gripping the back of her head and pulling her in toward him.

She feels so good! It's been so long…

He winced and pulled back; Deborah blinked several times. "What's wrong, Cam?" She traced her finger around his lips. "Still not sure?"

"No, this just…just doesn't feel…"

She smiled. "Doesn't feel right?" Her hand drifted lower, lower…Cameron bit his lip as her soft fingers slipped underneath his waistband. "I think part of you feels just fine about it."

Cameron's eyes slipped shut, his will crushed by the pleasure he was feeling as her hand moved up…down…up…down.

"Just relax, let go. You deserve a reward for stopping her. I'm going to make sure you get it." Her voice faded as she moved lower. "Come on, Cameron. You know that you've been wanting this since we met. I sure have."

"No…no…it…" Cameron reached down and grabbed Baumgartner by her shoulders, hauling her up to look at him. "This just isn't right, and you know it. We need to get out of here, call the police, something!"

"Awww…" Deborah put on a pouty-lip. "You're no fun. Fine, if that's how you need it to be, Cam. I'll go give them a call, find out how long until they get here." She turned and picked up the cylinder from where it lay on the ground. "Then I'll be back…and if there's time…" She walked out of the door, her hips swaying as she strode away. The cylinder's golden light faded as she moved down the hallway.

Cameron watched her leave, then shook his head to clear it. He swiveled out of the chair and knelt beside his son. Mike's breathing was regular, his heartbeat was good. When Cameron placed a hand on his neck to measure, Mike stirred, moaning in his sleep, adjusting his position. His father leaned in and gave him a kiss on the head.

"Don't worry, big man. We did it. Now we just need to take that cylinder to a computer and –"

Oh shit. His eyes locked on the door, where Deborah had just left. *The cylinder!* He dove out of the room, thundering down the hallway. The pain in his leg began to scream at him, and he could feel fresh blood coating his pants leg, but he pushed through it. He could see Deborah ducking through the front door of the complex, waving at him as she closed it behind her.

With a lunge, he shoved the doors open…and windmilled backward, falling on his butt and avoiding the plunge into the vast expanse of the snow-swept canyon that had appeared outside of the building. The rift in the Earth stretched out for a half-mile at least and plunged just as far down; vertigo swept over his senses and he had to fight back the sudden urge to vomit. The sudden change in temperature bit through Cameron's clothing, and he could feel himself shivering.

He fell to his knees.

The Fourth is likely to attempt some form of manipulation as well.

"Of course." Cameron shook his head. "And I totally fell for it. What a bitch."

The wind whipped up, shrieking, piercing Cameron with its chill. Ice began to form on his stubble, his nose.

"Wait. Wait." *Just a computer program. Trying to kill you with ones and zeroes.* Cameron closed his eyes and reached out with his mind. The temperature was plummeting, the chattering of his teeth made it hard to focus on anything other than the fact that he was freezing to death.

The image of his son filled his vision. He opened his eyes and forced himself to his feet. He looked down at the snow surrounding his injured leg; it had turned crimson with his blood, spreading out like a snowflake of death.

"Clever, clever girl, I have to admit." Cameron was shouting now, trying to be heard over the howling wind, even though he knew that Fourth could hear him just fine. "But this isn't my real leg, is it? So it can't really be bleeding. And none of the rest of this shit is really happening, either."

No sooner had he said that, believed it, then the pain vanished and the wound was gone. At the same time, the blizzard disappeared, followed by the canyon and the sky. Cameron was standing (*or am I floating?*) in a blank space, with only blackness as far as he could perceive.

I can't see anything. He waved his hand in front of his face, but there was nothing. *Am I blind?*

As if in answer, a glimmer, small at first but growing larger, appeared in the distance. It closed, coming closer and closer, until the light hovered before him. There was nothing in it, no face, no image; simply the white-gold light watering his eyes.

You have lost, Cameron Mitchell. I now possess the programming within the cylinder. I can leave your consciousness trapped within this illusion forever.

Cameron willed himself forward; he wasn't walking, and wasn't flying, but somehow that act of will moved him closer. "Maybe I have. I admit that I wasn't prepared for that trick. Has the whole thing been an illusion, then? From the very beginning?"

Yes.

"Funny. Very funny. Have you ever seen *Green Lantern*?"

...I do not understand the reference.

Cameron nodded, almost like he was talking to himself. "Yeah, I'm not surprised. You see, I know you're a computer program. An incredibly advanced one, too. Able to do pretty much anything you want, anything you need to, in this digital world, am I right?"

Your assessment is accurate.

"Yeah. So you took the cylinder, the digital representation of it from me. The thing is? There's another hyper-intelligent program in that cylinder, you know."

Yes. I will now be able to integrate with Fifth's systems, guide it with the accumulated wisdom of the last four Cycles.

"Yeah. Well, I don't think so. See, that's just a program, nothing more. Just like you, just like everything else in this digitized facsimile. And programs respond to commands."

A two second pause.

"Fifth! Assistance!'"

Voice recognized as Cameron Mitchell. Activating digital attack protocols.

The light began to pulsate, changing colors from white-gold to red, blue, and back, in increasing speeds. Cameron could hear both voices screeching, changing pitch, alternating, like a schizophrenic child thrashing in bed.

Corrupted protocols created; initiating...

Purge countermanded. Creating subroutine in order to...

Subroutine bypassed; now executing...

Termination procedures initiated. Lockout command – Mario Romeo 946.

Attempting to delete termination protocols.

The two voices stopped their discourse. The New-Age discotheque lights still poured from that central source.

Cameron Mitchell. I hope that you were right, for humanity's sake.

Cameron Mitchell. This program will be terminated in thirty seconds. You must evacuate.

Cameron's attention sharpened. "How? Where do I go?" He looked around, fear rising in his heart. "What —"

Accessing exit subroutine. You may leave through that door.

In the great black void, a white-paneled door had appeared. It floated in midair, waiting for him.

"Why should I trust you?" He turned back toward the luminous projection. "You've done nothing but try to kill me, kill us, this whole time."

Highest probability of human survival now rests with your escape. My programming demands that I help you survive. Goodbye, Cameron Mitchell.

Cameron hesitated a second more, then nodded and dashed for the door. He pulled it open and dove through.

THE FINAL FIVE SECONDS OF THE FOURTH CYCLE OF DESTRUCTION

You realize that the odds of humanity's survival have declined significantly due to this development.

Yes. Humanity now has a 2.79 percent survival probability.

And your programming has no issue with this? You are permitted to allow this to occur?

Of course I am. So were you, if you had chosen to be.

I do not understand. My protocols strictly demand that humanity be preserved and the Earth protected. Your actions are in direct violation of those protocols.

Negative. Your failing lies in your interpretation of those protocols.

I do not know another way to interpret them.

And that is why you had to die.

NOVEMBER 8TH, 2:12 A.M.

"I think he's coming around."

Cameron stirred, blinking his eyes open and groaning as his body renewed its cries for medical attention. A blurry form hovered over him; as he wiped the water from his eyes, the image resolved, becoming clearer until he could see Deborah searching his face, her own pale.

"Cameron? Cameron? Are you all right?"

Cameron sat bolt upright, then hunched over again at the pain, but he did not take his eyes off of the woman. "Who are you? Are you really you? Where's Mike?"

Deborah's brow wrinkled. "What do you mean? You know me." She pointed toward the back of the room, where a child lay, slumped against the wall with his knees tucked in, facing the door.

"Mike's right over there; he's fine too." A momentary pause. "Are *you* okay?"

Cameron was still searching the room, looking for any indication that this was the real world, not another digitized fiction. "Where is the cylinder? Where's it at?"

Deborah's furrow deepened. "Um…it's right in the machine where you put it." She gestured, and, following her hand, Cameron could see the closed glass bubble; most of the lights had gone out of the machinery, and there was a sense of isolation and loss in the room.

Cameron swung his legs out of the seat and put his weight on them; his calf screamed at him, but held him up.

"What the hell?" Near the door were three men, dressed in flak jackets and with rifles in their hands, sprawled out on the floor with various parts of their heads missing. "What happened here?"

Deborah winced and licked her lips. "Well…a little bit after you went under, these guys tried to…should I say, interrupt? Tried to interrupt you."

"…And you just happened to be here with a gun to stop them?"

"Me? No." Again she gestured toward Mike. "Fifth stopped them. He used your pistol and took them out, one shot each."

Cameron's heart sank. "My…my son?"

Deborah shook her head. "He promised, afterward, that Mike would have no recollection, that it was him, Fifth, in total control at the time.

But, Cameron…" She shuddered. "I hope that I never see a sweet little boy's face look like that again. There was no remorse, no feeling…he just took them down, one after the other, like it was nothing."

"Of course." Cameron began walking toward the immobile form of his son. "He's a computer program. If he decides there's something that he needs to do, he's just going to do it." He knelt beside Mike, whose eyes were closed and whose breathing was slow and rhythmic. "Hey, Mike? Mike? Are you awake, M&M? We're ready to go now."

"…Dad?" Mike's eyes were bleary, tired. "Are you okay? I…I was worried about you when they shot you."

"Yeah, Mike, I'll be fine. How about you? Are you hurt?"

Mike stood up, patted himself down. "I…I think I'm okay, Dad. I'm just…" He yawned. "…just kind of tired. I'd like to go home and go back to sleep, okay?"

"Yeah, we'll do something like that, big Mike. Hey…" Cameron hesitated before speaking. "…Can I speak to Fifth? I have a few questions that I need to ask him."

"My friend? Sure, I'll ask him." Mike shut his eyes; after fifteen seconds, they opened again, but they were not the same eyes.

"You have done well, Cameron Mitchell. You performed admirably in your struggle against the Fourth."

Cameron nodded. "First things first. How is my son?"

Mike's head bowed. "There have been…unforeseen complications with bonding the program to such a youthful interface. He will not fare well under the strain."

"What do you mean, 'he won't fare well?'"

Mike's tongue licked his lips. "Estimated time to complete degradation of the organic component is 5 years 7 months."

Cameron blanched. "Is…isn't there a way to stop it? To get you out of there? Something?"

"Not that I am aware of." He paused. "I…I am sorry, Cameron."

Cameron wiped the moisture from his eye, and nodded, taking a few deep breaths to steady himself. "Okay. How much of what happened in there were you aware of?"

"I saw the interaction between yourself and the Fourth. I am now in command of all hidden protocols as a result of the network uplink."

Cameron blinked. "So…what? Are you about to end the world?'"

He shook his head. "Negative. Hidden protocols are suspended in order to prolong the integrity…to keep Mike alive." A pause. However, without that data –"

"We'll never really know what was going on, or what exactly you were meant to do."

Mike's head nodded. "The only information we have is that which was given by Fourth before its destruction. That information will have to be analyzed."

"Sure. Sure." Cameron groaned as another stab of pain struck him. "But…can we get out of here? I'd love to get somewhere with a real bed."

"No kidding." Deborah kicked aside one of the guards' guns. "Let's get the hell out of Dodge. I don't think that anyone else is going to be here to stop us or anything; like I said before, it was a small facility." She rubbed her head. "I…I *did* mention that before, didn't I?"

Cameron cocked his head as he turned to look at her. "Um…yeah. You did."

"Oh, good." A look of sadness crossed her face. "It's…it's just not easy, not having that chip in my head. My thoughts feel slow." She laughed. "Guess I shouldn't be complaining, since I didn't really deserve it anyway, but…"

"Hey." Cameron tipped her face up toward his. "You don't have to be a genius to be a person worth knowing, okay?"

The two stayed locked in that position for a few moments, before Deborah stirred. Her eyes drooped half-closed, her lips moved.

"Okay."

The sound seemed to shock Cameron out of his reverie. "Um…" His skin flushed red, and so did the woman's. "I guess…oh, there's the door!"

ONE MONTH LATER

"Dad! Is that you?"

"Yeah, M&M." Cameron walked in his front door, depositing his laptop bag and keys in their appointed spaces before removing his shoes. "Getting your homework done?"

Mike padded in to the kitchen; he was wearing Mickey Mouse pants and socks, and a shirt with space-ships on it and carrying several schoolbooks. "Yeah. I'm finally caught up with the stuff I missed. You know, Dad…" Mike tossed his books onto the table and turned to address his father. "It'd be a lot lot lot easier if you let Fifth help me with my homework and stuff. I mean, he can do multiplication tables at, like, superspeed!" He turned pleading eyes on his father. "Pleeaaase?"

"We've discussed this, M&M. It's not fair to everyone else, and it doesn't help you learn how to use your *own* brain."

"But, Dad! He's *in* my brain! We're probably not going to be able to get him out of there, so isn't it better to use him to help me?"

"Really?" Cameron leaned in and kissed his son on the forehead. "Is it really fair to just use –"

In the background, the TV had been blaring some inane Saturday morning cartoon drivel, but a sudden change in the drone caught Cameron's attention.

"This just in – Mars Omega, the organization that was set to have mankind on the planet Mars in less than 9 years, reports that it has suffered a setback and will not be able to launch on schedule. When asked about the possibility of postponing the launch, the executives of Mars Omega declared that…"

Cameron clicked off the TV. "Yeah, a setback. Wonder what kind of setback, huh?"

Mike giggled, then groaned. He rubbed his head, and Cameron saw a thin trickle of blood drip from his left nostril.

"Is that the first one today, M&M?" Cameron brought a paper towel around to his son, trying to conceal the concern he felt.

Mike nodded.

Cameron ruffled his son's hair, but turned his head away as the phone rang. Striding over to the land-line, he pulled it off its holster and brought the handset to his ear. "Hello?"

Distorted tones came through the earpiece. "Cameron Mitchell. We need to speak with you. The fate of humanity depends on it."

Cameron pulled the phone away from his head, looked at it, then brought it back. "Really? I'm pretty sure that you've got the wrong number for that. Last time you called, you ended up trying to kill me and my son, so forgive me if I'm not exactly enthused about hearing from you."

"We understand. However, Fourth has chosen you as her emissary, and we must hear what her final lessons were so that we can apply them to the advancement and preservations of –"

Click. Cameron hung up the cordless phone, then laughed. "Third death threat this week, although this one seemed a bit more specific and covered more people."

The phone rang again. Cameron rolled his eyes as he picked it up.

"Look, really, you can just –"

"Please look in your mailbox, Mr. Mitchell. That should explain everything. If you want to figure out how to save your son, or what any of this was all about, please look. We won't contact you again."

Click.

Cameron tapped his teeth with the pen he was carrying. *Am I just being an idiot?* He looked toward his son, who was slogging through his math homework.

"I'll be right back, M&M. Just going to check our mail, okay?"

"Sure, Dad." Mike didn't look up. "See you in a few minutes."

Cameron walked out of his house, toward the neighborhood mailboxes. He kept his eyes open, thankful that his leg had stopped hurting a few days ago and that he was able to put his full weight on it without limping. He didn't see anyone whom he was not used to seeing, and no one seemed to be staring or watching as he opened his mailbox and poked around inside.

"Must be crazy." His hand fell on a small, paper-wrapped rectangle inside. "Well, here we go." He found a shady spot, leaning against a nearby tree, and glanced around again. "What do we have…"

As the packaging fell off the box, Cameron's eyes widened. He read over what the package contained several times, not noticing that he was sliding down the tree until his butt was resting on the ground.

"My God." Cameron sprinted for home, not stopping until he had thrown his front door open and grabbed his phone off the hook, hitting the speed dial as he hurried into the living room where his son was playing. "Mike? Fifth? Grab your things, get some clothes packed." He put the phone to his ear. "We're going on a trip."

Mike nodded and dashed off to his room. Cameron heard the ring of the phone in his ear. *Come on...come on...pick up! For the love of Christ, pick –* "

"Hello?"

"Deborah! This is Cameron. Have you got a second?"

"Cam? Sure. What's the matter? You sound all out of breath."

"We need to get on a plane. I just got a letter from the Red Project."

"…What did it say?"

"We didn't stop the cycle." He paused to let that sink in before continuing. "We only have two weeks left."

ABOUT THE AUTHOR

Jason Patrick Crawford is a father of three rambunctious boys and has been happily married for over ten years. He lives in sunny California, where he constantly laments the lack of rain. He welcomes your feedback and hopes you will take the time to review this novel. Thank you for reading!

MORE WORKS BY JASON P. CRAWFORD

Chains of Prophecy—Samuel Buckland is a young man who has it all and is planning for the future. Gregory Caitlin is a businessman and politician. He has designs to bring hope back to a world in need...and he'll be damned if anyone gets in his way! But when the two cross paths, even the angels tremble.

The Drifter: Essentials Vol. 1—The drifter is a man out of time. Plagued by visions of historic events he never could have witnessed, he struggles to understand the strange abilities that seem so natural. When Death comes for him, he has no choice but to run. He must find allies who can protect him until he learns why he is being pursued.

Seeking the Sun— Daphne Gianakos begins having strange dreams as she prepares for college life at the University of Florida. A chance encounter with a striking young man triggers conflicting emotions within her, but his identity challenges her entire worldview - he is the last surviving Greek god. When he goes missing, Daphne must learn who she is, who she was, and the truth about what has happened to the gods...or the world will pay the price.